"My sister has a daughter, a little girl named Katie."

"A little girl. How do you feel about that?" Mason asked, thinking he could predict Lisa's response all too well. No wonder she was chewing her lip. The dream of finding her birth family had *not* included a niece.

"I'm an aunt, and it's...I guess it's different. I never expected to be an aunt."

Given that she'd babysat only once in her entire life—an upsetting experience, as he recalled—he doubted she'd be willing to have much to do with the child. "I assume you plan to meet Katie," he said.

Lisa looked him straight in the eye, making it impossible for him to miss the hope in her expression. "No, it's a lot more than that. Katie needs me. I'm bringing her home."

Dear Reader,

There are few experiences in life as special as reading letters from those of you who have benefited from my books. So many of you wrote to say you identified with Emily Martin and her very personal loss in *Baby in Her Arms*. Your praise and appreciation made me realize that being able to write a story is a gift that reaches out to so many people in a very personal way.

This next book, *A Child Changes Everything*, was inspired by the idea that at some point in our lives as parents we experience a moment when we're unsure whether or not we're good parents.

Lisa Clarke's journey from being a fearful, hesitant parent to her discovery of what joy there is in being a mother forms the basis of *A Child Changes Everything*. Equally important to Lisa's story is Mason Stephens, the man she once loved, a man who comes to understand what it took for Lisa to bring Katie into her life. Their shared love for children rekindles their love for each other.

It is my hope that *A Child Changes Everything* will enrich your reading experience.

I welcome any feedback you might like to offer on this book, or any of my books. Please contact me on my Web site, www.stellamaclean.com, or e-mail me at stella@stellamaclean.com.

Sincerely,

Stella MacLean

A Child Changes Everything
Stella MacLean

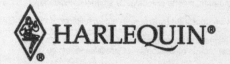

TORONTO • NEW YORK • LONDON
AMSTERDAM • PARIS • SYDNEY • HAMBURG
STOCKHOLM • ATHENS • TOKYO • MILAN • MADRID
PRAGUE • WARSAW • BUDAPEST • AUCKLAND

Recycling programs
for this product may
not exist in your area.

ISBN-13: 978-0-373-71655-5

A CHILD CHANGES EVERYTHING

ABOUT THE AUTHOR

Stella MacLean has spent her life collecting story ideas, waiting for the day someone would want to read about the characters who have lurked in her heart and mind for many years. Stella's love of reading and writing began in grade school and has continued to play a major role in her life. A longtime member of Romance Writers of America and a Golden Heart Award finalist, Stella enjoys the hours she spends tucked away in her office with her Maine coon cat, Emma Jean, and her imaginary friends while writing stories about love, life and happiness.

Books by Stella MacLean

HARLEQUIN SUPERROMANCE
1487—HEART OF MY HEART
1553—BABY IN HER ARMS

This book is dedicated to single parents everywhere, for the love and courage they show their children as they go about their daily lives.

ACKNOWLEDGMENTS

To Paula Eykelhof and Adrienne Macintosh, my editors, whose generous editorial support enriched this book in so many ways.

To Megan Long, editorial assistant, for all her thoughtfulness.

To my husband, Garry, whose unstinting encouragement made writing this book a wonderful process.

CHAPTER ONE

LISA CLARKE'S LIFE as she'd known it had ended.

She missed her mother; she especially missed the quiet evenings they'd shared these past few months, when they talked about her dad and her mother's early years in the family home in Durham, North Carolina. Her mother had kept that house because she loved it, the house Lisa still lived in today. It was during those evenings that her mom had confided her dream of playing professional tennis, a dream she'd left behind when she married Lisa's father. It was so like her mother to put her marriage first.

They'd been closer in those last months than at any time before, and Lisa was so thankful for all of it.

Today's meeting with Sherman Tweedsdale, the family lawyer, about her mother's will should be short and to the point. Other than a couple of bequests, she was the sole beneficiary.

Having given her name to his secretary, Lisa sat alone in the reception area. She didn't mind waiting for Tank, as her parents had always called him. She had only an empty house to go back to, and pressure from a real-estate agent to sell the property.

She'd spent an hour this morning making a list of things she needed to have done should she decide to put the property up for sale. She'd learned the list-making habit from her mom. She sighed. It all felt too soon. There were so many good memories of her life in that house, memories she wasn't prepared to abandon so quickly. True, her mom and dad had often been overprotective, but Lisa had realized long ago that their protection came from their love for her.

Relieved to have a few quiet moments to herself, she glanced around the paneled walls, her gaze coming to rest on a group of photos showing Tank's achievements. Staring at a photo of her father and Tank at a Chamber of Commerce awards dinner, Lisa became aware of someone approaching the reception area.

Shifting her gaze, she saw Mason Stephens standing there. The room dipped and swayed before it settled back, and still he stood there, his long black hair almost touching the neck of his dark leather jacket. Pain circled her heart, draining the air from her lungs.

Attempting to hide her dismay, she stared at the man who'd walked out of her life five years ago. His eyes still held the same piercing quality, adding to the air of authority he carried so well. Lisa made an effort to block the rush of emotions his presence exposed. She toyed with her purse strap and tried desperately to slow her racing pulse.

She could not let him see how much it hurt to be reminded of her own role in the failure of their relationship—her refusal to agree to children, a refusal Mason could never accept.

"Hello, Lisa," Mason said, his rueful smile lighting his gray-green eyes. Mason was a handsome man, and his good looks, combined with his self-assurance, made him every woman's dream. Or nearly every woman's...

"What are you doing here?" she asked, fighting to keep the tremor out of her voice as memories tumbled around her mind. Very often his evening shifts as a policeman and hers as a nurse had allowed them to meet at his apartment where they'd relax over a late supper. It was their special time together. She couldn't forget the excitement of being with him.

Despite the fluttering sensation in her stomach, she squared her shoulders and waited for his answer.

"I'm here to meet Tank," he said as he continued to look her over from his vantage point near the door.

Part of her wanted to bask in his appraising glance, but she couldn't afford to succumb to his well-honed charms; she knew the emotional toll reliving the past would take. Five years ago she'd loved Mason and believed that he loved her, until the night he'd proposed at their favorite restaurant and talked about the children he wanted. She'd tried to explain that she wasn't ready to have a family. But he hadn't understood and instead had said hurtful things before walking out of the restaurant and out of her life.

She'd seen Mason briefly at her father's funeral two years ago, as well as once at the grocery store with his then-wife, Sara, and their little boy. After that, she hadn't seen him again until last month at her mother's funeral.

So much for staying friends—his idea, not hers.

Still, although she missed Mason after they broke up, not seeing him was easier in so many ways.

Their final argument had ended in a painful exchange that convinced Lisa she was better off without him.

But her mother would want her to be polite, to take the high road. "Thank you for coming to Mom's funeral. I really appreciated it."

"You're welcome."

The minutes stretched while Lisa struggled to think of something to say to the man she'd once loved.

"So, you've become a P.I. I saw the ad in the paper for your firm. A year ago you left the police force, wasn't it?" she said to ease the awkwardness between them.

Leaning against the door frame, he shoved his hands in the pockets of his sizzling-tight jeans. "Yeah, it's been a pretty hectic year all-around."

"How's Sara?"

His expression clouded over. "You really want to know?"

Why had she asked that? Thanks to Sara's sister Melanie, who was also a nurse and worked at the hospital with her, Lisa had heard that Mason's marriage had ended after a year. She wasn't interested in Mason's ex-wife, and she definitely did not want him to think she was.

But she had always thought Sara and Mason made sense as a couple and deep down she believed they'd get back together. After all, they shared common interests like a love of rock music, motorcycles—and they shared a son, while she and Mason hadn't been able to agree on something as fundamental as having children.

"Melanie hasn't mentioned Sara or her singing career for a while," she said, trying to explain the question to herself as well as him.

Mason shifted his weight from one foot to the other, his eyes dark. "Sara's doing fine—"

"Hello, there," Tank Tweedsdale said, giving Mason a friendly smile as he cruised into the room. "We'll just be a couple of minutes, Mason…if you want to wait here. Lisa, if you'll come with me." He beckoned her into his office and closed the door behind her.

She sat in one of the chairs facing Tank's desk, relieved that all this would soon be over.

Placing his briefcase beside his desk, he bent over

and kissed Lisa on the cheek, his goatee brushing her skin. "How are you doing, dear?" he asked, his kindly gaze searching her face as he took his own seat.

"I'm okay." She settled farther into her chair as Tank opened the file in front of him.

"Lisa," he began slowly, "you're aware that other than a couple of bequests to Duke University you're the sole beneficiary in your mother's will. I've filed all the documents necessary to finalize the estate. Your mother's stockbroker will be calling you in the next couple of days to go over your financial situation. You won't have any money worries."

She'd always known that her mom and dad had been careful investors, but money was the last thing on her mind. She nodded, waiting for him to continue.

Tank cleared his throat as he took a sheet of paper out of the file. "And of course you're aware that you're adopted."

Adopted? Why would Tank bring that up? He was the lawyer who'd arranged her adoption thirty years ago. She nodded again. "My birth parents died in a car accident."

Tank stared at the green banker's lamp on the corner of his desk before meeting her questioning gaze. "That's not completely true," he said, passing her the paper. She glanced at the page and recognized her mother's precise handwriting.

My Darling Lisa,

I've loved you since the moment you were placed in my arms. I have something to confess, and I pray you can understand that we did it because we loved you. We thought it best not to tell you that Carolyn Lewis didn't die in the car accident with your birth father, that she is still alive. A lawyer we know in Florida contacted us about a baby girl that needed a home. He said that because of the accident, your mother could no longer take care of you and had elected to put you up for adoption. After your dad passed away, I began to worry that you'd be left without any close family, and so I wanted to tell you about Carolyn Lewis.

But my biggest fear has always been that if I told you about your mother it would make you so upset that you'd never speak to me again. By the time you read this, it won't matter.

I hope you can forgive what your father and I have done. We should've told you, let you have a life with your birth mother, but we couldn't bring ourselves to share you with anyone. We loved you with all our hearts, and you were everything we ever wanted in a child.

I won't dwell on our reasons, or why we did what we did, as it's too late for regrets. Tank is prepared to help you find your birth mother.

Trust him, darling—he's a good man and a dear friend.
Love,
Mom

Shock and bewilderment made Lisa's heart pound against her ribs. Her throat tightened, warding off the sting of tears. "I don't understand. If my birth mother is still alive, why did they keep her from me? I had a right to know my mother, for heaven's sake!"

"Lisa, I'm sorry you had to learn about it this way, but your parents wouldn't take my advice to tell you themselves. They were very private people who lived for each other—and you."

Feeling betrayed by the two people she'd loved most in the world, Lisa turned on Tank. "What am I supposed to do now? How am I supposed to find my birth mother? And what if I have brothers and sisters and never had the chance to meet them? I don't get it. Why did Mom wait until now to tell me? I deserved better than that. I've been a good daughter. Everything they ever wanted me to do, I did—"

"Your mother agonized over this for months after she was diagnosed with cancer. Alice tried to tell you, but in the end, she couldn't do it. Finally, she asked that funds be set aside to see that Carolyn Lewis was found. If that's what you want…"

His words reminded her of all the times she'd imagined her birth parents and what they would've wanted for her, all the times she'd wished she could have met them.

And all the while, her mother had been alive.

"What I *want?* I want my family…my mother, anyone who can tell me who I am. My whole life I believed there was some terrible secret buried in my past."

Was there a dark secret involving her birth parents? Had they been criminals? Were they fugitives when her father died in the car accident? Why had no one come looking for her?

If there wasn't something to be ashamed of, why hadn't her adoptive parents told her Carolyn Lewis was alive? Why had they let her grow up without knowing the truth?

She'd often attempted to ask her mom and dad about her past, but each time they gave the same answer. There was no reason for her to concern herself with that sort of thing. This was always followed by their usual argument—they'd waited so long for her, they'd loved her before they'd even set eyes on her.

The desire to please her parents and to avert her mother's onslaught of tears at the mention of her birth parents had stopped Lisa from seeking answers. Their attitude had increasingly made her feel set apart, isolated in the midst of her parents' love.

"I can't explain their decision, Lisa, but I had to respect their wishes."

"All my questions could have been answered so easily."

"Yes, they probably could have, but the past can't be changed," Tank said gently.

Her voice thick with loss and longing for what might have been, she whispered, "So, my dad—my birth father—died in a car accident, right?"

Tank nodded. "Grant Lewis died in a collision, and your mother, Carolyn Lewis, is somewhere in Florida...we believe."

"Does Carolyn—I mean, my mother—know where I live?"

Tank sat up straighter. "Your parents didn't say. I arranged your adoption, but I don't have much information beyond the fact that your mother was in Florida at that time. I've taken the liberty of hiring Mason to find your mother."

"Mason?"

"Mason does my investigative work, and he's completely reliable," Tank said, a sheepish look in his clear blue eyes.

"Is Mason the right person to do this? He was a great cop, and I'm sure he's a good P.I...." But she couldn't care less about his credentials at the moment. She and Mason just didn't fit together, as lovers or as friends.

"Lisa, Mason's had a rough time with his old partner in the P.I. firm. He's had to start at the bottom and rebuild the business. He's worked hard."

"Yes, I heard about Stewart taking off with company money."

"Mason still has great contacts in the law-enforcement business. If you want to locate your mother as quickly as possible, he can do it for you. Trust me. I'll see to it that your interests are protected."

"You spoke to him before talking to me about this?" she asked, annoyed that she hadn't been consulted first but remaining polite. Being polite and courteous was her mother's legacy.

He nodded.

"I don't want Mason involved in my personal business." There were a dozen reasons she didn't want Mason around, beginning with the fact that he already knew too much about her.

"Lisa, I realize that you and Mason had your difficulties, but he will be discreet."

She sat there, the knowledge that her mother was still alive filtering through her mind, and suddenly felt hopeful, ready to take on her new circumstances.

If working with Mason meant finding her birth mother as quickly as possible, she was willing to ignore the past. Besides, Mason was a very capable investigator. *Better the devil you know,* she mused. "Are you sure Mason wants to do this?"

"Mason has agreed to start immediately, and the sooner the search is under way, the sooner you can meet your birth mother…. If you want to go ahead with it, that is."

Regardless of past differences, Mason *would* respect her privacy. "What matters most is finding my mother."

"Thatta girl," Tank said, relief evident on his face as he went to the door.

"Come in, Mason."

Mason walked to the chair next to Lisa and sat down, putting him within touching distance. But touching him was out of the question. She edged away.

She listened while Tank ran through the provisions of the will, including funds set aside for locating Carolyn Lewis. Yet it was as if they were talking about someone she had no real connection with—and she didn't. Not yet.

But that was a situation she planned to resolve, with or without Mason's help. Still, as she listened to Tank, she caught herself hoping that she and Mason *would* be able to work together. Mason had always been a man of his word, someone she could rely on. It was one of his best qualities, as far as her parents were concerned. And he'd made her feel safe, which had seemed so contradictory, given his pull-out-all-the-stops attitude toward life.

Seeing the concentration on his face, the way he was so comfortable in his own skin, his powerful hands resting on the arms of the chair, she was aware of how easy it would be to rely on him once again.

"This would be a professional relationship, nothing more," she told him after Tank had finished his explanation.

"What other kind of relationship is there?" he asked with the barest hint of a smile on his face.

Those words reminded her of other words, earlier words, spoken in another time and place, laced with anger and pain. "None that fits this particular situation," she said, tucking her arms against her body.

And yet, what they'd shared had been so special, so much a part of her dreams. When she'd been with Mason, everything had seemed possible. She didn't want to admit that she still felt tiny pinpricks of regret. Had they made a huge mistake in letting their relationship go?

No, Mason dared to dream big, take risks…and in the end, she couldn't see herself in a world like that.

He leaned toward her, his gaze direct, uncompromising. "Lisa, you don't have to worry. I will not let our past interfere with doing my job. You need my professional help, and you can depend on me to deliver."

Trapped by his gaze, she fought to hide her sadness that somehow their relationship had gone so wrong, so quickly. "I appreciate that," she said. "And I am counting on it."

MASON'S GUT ACHED seeing Lisa sitting there, so close yet out of reach. It hurt to hear her voice, so soft and sure, a voice that had once been a beacon of stability for him.

The blue of her eyes drew him into her space with the promise of how much she cared for those she loved—and a few years ago he'd been one of those lucky people.

Meeting her eyes, he reminded himself how different they were in their approach to life. How those differences had meant the end of their relationship.

She wanted certainty and being able to rely on a future bright with contented sameness. She didn't seem to have the capacity to cope with change. And nothing he'd said had altered her position.

He could finally admit that as he sat next to her.

Lisa's determination to maintain the status quo had been one thing, but it had been her refusal to consider having a family that had sounded the death knell for any future together.

He hadn't understood her back then and he still didn't. Lisa had every advantage in life, while he'd worked for everything he had. Yet she was afraid to take a chance on life, on him or anything outside her predictable world.

Meanwhile, he'd found a comfortable level of enjoyment, if not outright happiness, in his life after Lisa, even after his failed marriage. Despite the changes in his life, he'd often thought of her, if she'd found her own happiness without him.

But watching Lisa now forced him to admit how lonely she was, how much of an emotional blow learning about her birth mother had been. He'd been well aware of how deeply she'd yearned to know her birth parents, to be part of a family she could call her own, not those stiff-necked relatives on her mother's side.

When Tank had initially filled him in on the case, Mason had believed that Alice and Jim Clarke's actions were cruel, especially considering that they'd known better than anyone how lonely Lisa had been all these years.

Given the complication of his and Lisa's past and its potential influence on the case, he had wanted to turn down the job, but the sad truth was that he needed the money to get his business on a sound financial footing. He would hardly be seen as anybody's hero by including his financial welfare as part of his reason for taking Lisa's case. But he had to get his finances straightened out if he was going to be able to provide for his son, Peter.

And the retainer from Lisa's case would cover his agency's expenses for at least a month—enough time to expand his client list.

In addition to the advantages a cash retainer gave his struggling agency, there was another issue, a much more fundamental one. If Lisa had to learn bad news about her birth mother, he owed it to her to be the one to tell her. She probably wouldn't agree that he was the best person to do it, but seeing her brought forward feelings he'd never admitted to anyone. Not even to himself. When they were together, he'd wanted to be the one she turned to, the one she could trust. He'd blown it then, but now he had the chance to make it up to her.

Before he'd walked in here today he'd convinced himself he could handle this job. Sitting there now, seeing her obvious distress, made him a little less sure.

"Lisa, I won't take the case if it makes you uncomfortable."

She started to say something, then caught herself. "I want you to find my mother," she said, determination flowing through every word.

"I'll do whatever I can," he responded, seeing how tightly she gripped the arms of the chair. At least she wasn't doing her best to ignore him the way she had the few times they'd met over the past five years.

Lisa had been a dutiful, loving daughter to her parents, the same parents who'd let her down. Lisa's dedication to them was one of the reasons he'd been attracted to her in the beginning. Lisa had never failed to organize birthday parties for her mom and dad. She'd once told him that one of her reasons for becoming a nurse was to be there for them when they needed nursing care.

Although Lisa seemed to be accepting the loss of her mother quite well, Mason knew that deep down she had to be hurting. Easing her pain was another justification for doing what he could to help her.

"Thank you," she said.

Seeing the apprehension on her face, he ached to take her into his arms. But what would be the point? He didn't need the grief of revisiting an old relationship and all the mistakes lurking there. With Lisa, he'd made the kind of mistakes that couldn't be undone.

"Great. Now that Mason's on board, we're all set," Tank said. "Lisa, I'll keep you informed of Mason's progress on the case."

"So that's it? There's nothing left to do?" Lisa asked in a calm voice.

"Only to wait for Mason's report," Tank said, turning his attention to Mason.

Taking that as his cue to get on with the job, Mason stood. "I'll be in touch."

He'd almost made it to the door when he heard her.

"Mason, I need to speak to you."

Tank gave a nervous chuckle. "Then I'll leave you two young people alone." Tank was up and out the door before either of them could respond.

Lisa came toward Mason, her back straight. She was, as usual, immaculately groomed. Not a strand of her highlighted blond hair had escaped from her ponytail. Her pearl earrings matched her pearl-drop necklace. Her short black skirt showed off her legs as she moved.

"What can I do for you?" he asked, trying to ignore the memory of how right she felt in his arms, how the perfume she always wore made his blood run hot.

"When you locate my mother, I expect you to call me immediately. I want to see her as soon as I can."

Hope shone from her eyes, but Mason had worked in missing persons and knew the devastation hope could cause when the search turned sour.

"I understand how you feel, but have you considered that this might not be a positive experience? Maybe your parents didn't tell you about your birth mother for a good reason."

Shock darkened her eyes. She lifted her chin. "I don't care what the reasons are. If she's alive, I'm going to meet her."

He saw the purposeful set to her jaw, but pressed on, anyway. "Lisa, sometimes there are things we're better off not uncovering."

"Not in this case. If I'd been told about my mother, I would've found her years ago." She worked her fingers through the strap of her black leather bag, her eyes holding his. "My mother deserves to know who I am, what I've become. That I turned out just fine…without her."

Her voice dropped to an emphatic whisper. "I *need* to meet her."

He recognized something in her eyes he'd only seen when they'd talked about his chaotic life growing up in a family of six kids.

Naked longing.

"You're hoping you have a sister or a brother."

A whimper of protest slipped past her lips, and her eyes widened. "Please find my mother as soon as possible."

It wasn't as if he was flush with cases. And with that look in her eyes, it wouldn't have mattered, anyway. "I'll make this my priority."

He saw her reach for him, then pull back. He understood that her reaching out was an act of relief rather than any caring for him. But he'd taken away her reason to care with his impulsive behavior. He'd do what he could to support her through this. He owed her that much.

The breakup had been his fault because in his shock and anger at her insistence that she didn't want children he'd said some pretty nasty things about her selfishness, her stubbornness and the cold heart she had to have not to want to share her life with a child. He'd regretted his words afterward, but it was too late to take them back. He could never heal the hurt he'd seen in her eyes, and he'd never been able to erase that look from his mind. "Here's my business card and cell number. Call me anytime."

"Thank you," she said, and for the first time since he'd entered the room a smile raised the corners of her mouth.

As she turned to leave, Mason wished they could somehow connect, despite everything that had gone wrong between them. He needed her appreciation, her respect, as much now as he had back then.

Back when they'd loved each other, he had believed she could change—that loving Lisa the way he had would give her the courage to take a chance on their love, their future together.

He'd learned the hard way that Lisa Clarke wouldn't risk her emotionally safe way of life, regardless of what was at stake.

CHAPTER TWO

SEEING MASON HAD BEEN unsettling to say the least. Trying to overcome the crazy and confusing emotions his return to her life had created, Lisa spent the next two weeks, in between shifts at the hospital, working on all the estate paperwork and financial issues that still had to be dealt with.

Tank was right—money would not be a problem for her, which meant she was free to do whatever it took to locate her birth mother.

Despite her earlier misgivings, the idea that her mother might be out there somewhere filled her with excitement and hope for the future.

She missed her adoptive mother a great deal, but Alice's overprotective and fearful attitude had been a source of anxiety in Lisa's life.

Although Alice Clarke had never said it in so many words, Lisa had understood that as much as her mother loved her, she hadn't been at ease with raising her. Children were cause for concern. Children were accidents waiting to happen.

But what her adoptive mother had done or not done was in the past. The important thing now was to hear from Mason about Carolyn Lewis. How would it feel to see the woman who'd given birth to her? What would her mother look like and how would she sound?

There were moments she couldn't believe Carolyn was still alive. That the morning in Tank's office had been a dream.

When Alice became ill, Lisa had given up her apartment and moved home to manage her mother's care with the help of a home nurse. This morning, finding it difficult to sleep in her parents' empty house, Lisa went to work early for her day shift at Duke Medical.

Two years ago, she'd left her job as a nurse in the emergency department to go to the pediatric unit to better understand why children made her so anxious. Despite her initial fear she had been surprised at how much she enjoyed working in pediatrics. When a position had opened up for head nurse of the unit, she'd cranked up her courage and applied. A month ago she'd gone in for the interview and she was hopeful. If she got the job it would be proof that she could be responsible for a child—at least of their physical needs. Whether or not she could tend to their emotional needs by coming to grips with her own feelings was still unlikely. But it was a step in the right direction and she was proud of how far she'd gotten in the process.

Although she defended her decision not to have her

own children that night in the restaurant to Mason, his words had had an impact.

And her time in the pediatric ward had forced her to face the root of her anxieties. Sure, her mother had influenced how she behaved around kids, but the real reason was Linda Jean Bemrose and the night the little girl had nearly died when Lisa was babysitting. All because she'd been talking on the phone instead of watching Linda Jean.

"I didn't expect you to be here this early," Melanie Campbell said as Lisa entered the unit. "How are you doing?"

Lisa hadn't seen Sara's sister for a couple of weeks, due to different nursing rotations. "I'm doing quite well, really."

"You're sure? I was worried the pressure of caring for your mother and then going through the funeral might be too upsetting for you. If it were me, I'd be so tired." Melanie slumped down in her chair.

Lisa wished she could tell Melanie about her birth mother, but it would mean a whole lot of explaining she couldn't handle right now.

It embarrassed her that she felt she couldn't share something important in her life with a friend, but that was how private issues had been dealt with in her family. The only person she'd ever talked to about being adopted was Mason. He'd been so understanding when she'd told him how much she wished she'd known her birth parents. That confession had brought them closer—until that night at the restaurant. She wondered afterward if maybe he'd been looking for an excuse to break up with her; he'd never made an issue of children before that night. When she'd heard he'd married Sara a short time later, her suspicions were confirmed.

"It's been a difficult time," she said, "but each day gets a little easier."

"I have the perfect tonic for you. Sara's rock band is playing a Fourth of July concert right here in Durham, and I have two free tickets."

Sara's band wasn't her type of music. Lisa preferred light classical, but it was sweet of Melanie to offer her a ticket. "Thank you for thinking of me, but maybe another time."

Enthusiasm radiated from Melanie's brown eyes. "You're going to miss a great night. Sara said an L.A. talent agent is going to be at the July 4th show. She's already met him a couple of times and she's sure that he's going to offer her a contract." Her smile faded. "Then the band would have to move to L.A."

Mason and Sara were divorced, but what would happen if Sara took Peter away with her? How would Mason feel about that? But it was no longer her concern; besides, she needed to concentrate on her own life.

"Your sister's braver than I am. I wouldn't want to move away from here. Especially to a place like Los Angeles."

"Me, neither, but Sara's music career is important to her."

Lisa merely nodded but underneath her calm exterior, she felt a strange sense of loss. Regardless of how he'd behaved with her, she'd always known what family meant to Mason. He would want Peter to be around people who loved him, especially Mason's large family.

HOURS LATER, WEARY BUT feeling good about her workday, Lisa parked by her house. As she entered, she was acutely aware of the silence. Without the sounds of the TV and the caregiver chatting and playing cribbage with her mother, the house had no life.

On nights like this the idea of listing the house made sense to her. She put her keys and purse on the granite counter and slipped her arms out of her jacket.

As she'd done for the past two weeks, she checked for messages, and this time there was one—from Mason. He was in Florida and wanted her to call him on his cell.

Barely able to contain her excitement, she dialed the number. Mason answered on the first ring. "Thanks for getting back to me," he said.

She clutched the phone. "You found my mother."

"I did. Carolyn Lewis is in a nursing home outside Melbourne."

Carolyn Lewis. Her mother. Despite all the times she'd imagined meeting her, she was suddenly overcome with dread at the prospect.

"Is she okay? What did she say when you told her I was looking for her?"

There was a long pause.

"What's wrong? Mason, please, if there's a problem, I need to know. Is she okay?" Then a thought struck her. "Is my mother ill?"

"No, she seems all right, Lisa. But I didn't talk to her. That's up to you. How soon can you get down here?"

If she could trade a couple of shifts... "I'll be there the day after tomorrow. Where exactly are you?"

"Have you got a pen handy?"

She searched the kitchen drawer, unearthing a pen and pad of paper from under the material the real-estate agent had left her. "Go ahead."

He gave her the address of Carolyn's nursing home and the hotel where he was staying.

"I'll call you as soon as I've made arrangements with the hospital," she said. It might mean asking for more time off, but whatever it took, she'd be on the road the day after tomorrow. "Mason, one last thing—"

"You'd like to know if you have any other family.

I can't answer that, but if it'll help, I'll go with you when you visit her."

Had he discovered something in Melbourne that he didn't want to tell her over the phone? He'd warned her that she might not like what she found out, hadn't he? She held the phone even tighter.

Could she face this on her own? When her father had died she'd had her mother, and when her mother had become ill and then passed away, she'd had her mother's caregiver and her friends. But now she felt very much alone and unequipped to deal with everything.

Mason was the only person she knew in Florida. Having him with her *would* make it easier.

"I'd appreciate it if you'd go with me," she said, taking a deep breath.

"You got it. I'll be waiting for you," he said, his reassuring voice comforting her.

Two days later, Lisa stood beside Mason outside the Palmetto Bayside Nursing Home, her hands clammy as she tried to quell her anxiety. She'd driven most of the night to get from North Carolina to Florida. During the long hours, she'd been consumed by one idea—what if her mother hadn't contacted her in all these years because she didn't want to see her?

But how could she *not* want to see her daughter? Lisa didn't say the words out loud. Mason already felt sorry for her; it had been in his eyes, which was more than enough reason not to confide in him. "How do I tell her who I am?"

"Lisa, you just got into town thirty minutes ago. Why don't we come back a little later after you've had a chance to relax and think about how you want to handle this?" Mason's gentle tone was in stark contrast to his assessing gaze.

She'd thought of nothing else in the final hours before she turned off I-95. "No, it has to be now." *Before I lose my nerve.*

A frown formed on Mason's face. "Okay, here's what we'll do. I'll wait outside the room while you go in. If you need me, come to the door."

"Thank you." She was aware of the tremor in her voice as she spoke.

"You'll be okay," he said encouragingly, placing his hand on the small of her back as they walked to the main entrance together.

After they checked in at the reception desk, the aide assigned to her mother led them down the corridor to Carolyn Lewis's room. The hallway was narrow and cluttered with wheelchairs and walkers. The paint on the walls was chipped and marked, and a faint scent of baby powder and stale urine hung in the air.

At the door, the aide entered and Mason stepped back, allowing Lisa to follow. "I'll be right here," he whispered.

Apprehension rushed through her. She turned her face up to his. "Wish me luck."

He winked at her. "Good luck."

Clasping her purse with both hands, she walked in. At first, she wasn't sure which of the two people was her mother. One woman sat in a wheelchair by the window, while the other lay on her bed, muttering to herself as she read the paper. Lisa hesitated.

"Mrs. Lewis, you've got a visitor," the aide said, moving toward the woman in the wheelchair.

Lisa inched forward, her heart thudding. The woman shifted in her chair, pain skidding across her face at the movement. Her gaze was direct as she looked up at Lisa. "Who are you?"

"I'm Lisa."

"No… It can't be. Lisa, is that really you?" Carolyn extended her hands, her long, bony fingers quivering. "Tell me I'm not dreaming."

Lisa's mouth was suddenly dry. "You're not. I'm Lisa, your daughter."

Joy lit her mother's expression, her face transformed by a smile as Carolyn Lewis's eyes roved slowly over Lisa. "You look so much like your father," she murmured.

Relieved that her mother recognized her, Lisa slid into the chair beside her. "I look like my dad," she whispered. Happiness brought a smile to her face as she took her mother's hand. She wanted to laugh and cry at the same time. Moving closer, she kissed her mother's cheek.

"Yes, there's so much of your father in you. He had high cheekbones, too—very aristocratic. You have his blue eyes and blond hair."

Gently she touched Lisa's hair. "Oh, my darling daughter, I've wanted to meet you for so long. You have no idea what it's like to live in hope that one day you'll see your little girl again," she said, a smile trembling on her lips.

Words abandoned Lisa as she met her mother's eager gaze.

Carolyn appeared much older than Lisa had envisioned. With her gray-streaked hair pulled up in a bun and her face devoid of any makeup, she looked aged, worn-out. As much as she hated herself for doing it, Lisa couldn't help comparing Carolyn with her immaculately groomed adoptive mother, who had never missed a hair or manicure appointment.

Yet as she sat there, studying this woman who held her past, the words slipped out. "Why didn't you come for me? Why did you leave me alone all these years? I needed you—"

Carolyn softly stroked Lisa's cheek, her eyes alight with love and caring. "I couldn't. I promised your parents I wouldn't try to contact you if they'd provide a good life for you."

"But why did you give me up? Surely you had family to turn to after my dad died."

"I had no brothers or sisters, and my parents were gone. My sister-in-law, your aunt Helen—God rest her soul—did what she could to help me."

Her mother pulled Lisa's hands into her lap. "Let me explain. I was four months pregnant when we had the accident. Your father died after a week in the hospital, and I nearly lost you from the trauma. Then I spent months trying to regain the use of my legs."

"I'm so sorry," Lisa said, squeezing her mother's fingers.

"They were expensive months, and not only that, I suffered permanent physical damage. I couldn't pay the hospital bills or put bread on the table. Even with insurance there were still extra medical bills to pay, plus funeral expenses, and we had very little in savings. I would've found a way to keep you if I'd been able to work, but it wasn't possible."

Overcome with a sense of regret, Lisa glanced away, her eyes coming to rest on several photographs that stood on the windowsill behind her mother. "Do I have…family?"

"You have an older sister, Anne Marie." Her mother reached for a framed photo on the window ledge and passed it to Lisa. Smiling at the camera was a tall woman with short brown hair and glasses, wearing a yellow tank top and shorts.

A sister. I have a sister. Delight tugged at her as she picked up the photo, searching for clues about her sister. "What's she like? Where does she live? What kind of music does she listen to? Does she play sports? I'm hopeless at anything but tennis," she admitted, eager to learn everything she could about her sister.

"Anne Marie played basketball in high school."

Lisa held the picture in unsteady hands, fighting back hurt that her mother had somehow managed to keep in touch with Anne Marie and not her. "What happened to Anne Marie? Where did she live after the accident?"

"Anne Marie was five when your father died. I was afraid that if I approached an agency, they'd take her from me because I couldn't care for her, and I'd never see her again. I couldn't lose both my children—" She choked on the words.

"If your aunt Helen hadn't taken Anne Marie, I don't know what I would've done. As it turned out, I got word that a lawyer in Tampa who knew Mrs. Clarke had found a home for you. The lawyer told me that your parents couldn't have children and they wanted to adopt a baby girl. With no money coming in except social security—which didn't even cover the cost of my medical bills—I had to believe you'd be better off with a couple with the money to give you what you needed. I wouldn't have let you go with them if I'd had any choice."

"Why couldn't Aunt Helen raise me?" Lisa asked,

unwilling to think that giving her up had been that simple.

"She was divorced with very little income, and she had two toddlers of her own. Besides, if you had the chance to have every advantage in life, at least I could give you that opportunity," her mother said, voice shaking. "I wanted you to have what I'd never be able to provide for you. The doctors told me my legs would never be right again, which meant I couldn't earn a living. Anne Marie was about to start kindergarten when Grant died. I was afraid she would be traumatized by being taken away from her mother, her home. You were just a baby, you wouldn't remember any other life but the one you had with the Clarkes. If I could have kept you both, I would have. But look around you, what kind of life would you have had here with me?"

"Did you ever try to contact me, to see if I was doing okay? You didn't just let me go, did you? How could you do that?" Lisa asked, holding her loneliness at bay. "I *wanted* you. I *needed* to know who you were, who I was."

Tears pooled in Carolyn's eyes as her voice sputtered. "I… It—it was a long time ago, and I made a promise to your parents. For the most part, I kept that promise so I wouldn't cause trouble for you."

Lisa bit back a sharp retort. What good would it do to take out her anger on this woman who was convinced she'd done the right thing? "I wish—"

"Look here," Carolyn said, her face suddenly suffused with excitement. "I have something to show you." She turned her wheelchair to the window and picked up a black-and-while photo in a silver frame. "Do you remember this?"

Lisa took the photo, staring at it in disbelief. It was a picture of her standing with a girl she had met that unforgettable day in front of Smiley's hot-dog stand. "We were vacationing in Myrtle Beach. I was eight. My mother didn't want me near the water. She was afraid I'd drown. But Dad let me go, and I met this girl on the beach. We played together most of the afternoon."

She smiled at the memory. "I was so pleased that someone older was willing to play with me and treated me like a big kid. We had a great time in the water. I'll always remember that day. Her name was Mary. How did you get this?"

Her mother touched the picture lovingly. "Despite my promise not to see you after you were adopted, I got a friend of mine to check the telephone listings for every Clarke in Florida, Georgia and the Carolinas. Just before your eighth birthday, I located your parents and called them. Your mother was very upset. She reminded me that I'd agreed not to see you or be involved in your life, and if I called again, she'd have her husband, a district attorney, take action to protect you from me."

"My mother said that?" Lisa asked, shocked to learn Alice Clarke could do something so cruel.

"In the conversation she let it slip that they were taking you to Myrtle Beach for your birthday. My situation hadn't changed, I still couldn't care for you. But I had to know that you were being well treated, that you were happy. I was frantic to see you. I didn't dare make the trip because I wasn't well, but mostly because I couldn't trust myself not to talk to you and break my agreement with your parents."

"So, what did you do?"

She sat back in her wheelchair, her gaze locked on Lisa's face, her eyes bright. "Helen agreed to go and make sure you were okay. A reporter friend of hers had found a photo of your father in the Durham newspaper. I still have the clipping. Helen and I saved every spare penny so she could make the trip with Anne Marie and her kids. She intended to watch for your father and get a quick snapshot of you. You can imagine her pleasure when you and Anne Marie struck up a friendship. She took this picture for me so I could see what a beautiful child you were."

"And all that time my sister and my cousins were there and I had no idea," Lisa said, her heart opening to the love in her mother's eyes. Her mother had never given up on her; she'd been there in secret, loving her and needing to make sure she was all right.

"This photo of you playing with Anne Marie—

we called her Mary when she was little—has been a constant source of comfort to me."

"For weeks after that trip to Myrtle Beach, I begged my parents to let me invite Mary to come for a visit. But somehow it never happened... Could my parents have known who Anne Marie was?"

"Helen didn't think so, which was a huge relief to both of us. If they'd recognized her somehow, I'm sure I would have heard from their lawyer about breaking my promise. Anyway, none of it matters now. You're here and my prayers have been answered."

"My sister and I spent a day at the beach together, and neither of us knew who the other one was?"

Carolyn nodded, a sweet smile on her face. "Helen didn't tell Anne Marie who she was playing with... yet it was so like your sister to be kind to younger children."

"My aunt Helen was aware of who I was and said nothing?"

"I've always wondered how Helen managed to keep my secret from Anne Marie."

"Anne Marie doesn't know about me?"

"No, I never told her. When I was pregnant, we had talked with Anne Marie about her new sibling, but she didn't really understand. So when I decided to give you up, I thought it best for the Clarkes to take you straight from the nursery and I would explain if she asked or when she was older. But with her life in such upheaval, she didn't ask, and as time went on it just got more difficult to bring up the subject."

"What about after the trip to Florida? Why not say something then?"

A look of regret crossed Carolyn's face as she whispered, "I thought about it, but if she'd realized who you were, she might have gone to your parents later on and…caused problems for you."

She and Anne Marie had both been robbed of so many experiences. How she wished she could have known her sister all these years. Not having the opportunity to share her childhood with her made Lisa even more determined to make up for lost time. She had a sister whom she'd loved with all her young heart that sun-filled day on the beach. "I really liked her. She was so accepting, so much fun. To think I played for hours with my *sister*… Where is she? I want to meet her."

Pulling her hands from Lisa's, Carolyn drew back, pain and heartache in the lines of her face. She swallowed, her hands working nervously in her lap. "Anne Marie was arrested two days ago. She's in jail."

CHAPTER THREE

TAPPING THE WALL impatiently, Mason waited for Lisa to come out of her mother's room. The old need to protect her welled up in him, making him restless. He was very conscious of the fact that they were no longer involved, yet seeing Lisa's anxiety over meeting her mother had bothered him more than he'd expected.

As he stood there, he wondered how they'd ever ended up together. Before he'd met her, he'd boasted to his buddies that there wasn't a woman alive who could hold him, which was the truth—until the day he stood across the gurney from Lisa, the emergency room nurse caring for his mother, who'd broken her arm.

For the first time, he'd found himself speechless with a woman. And he hadn't the faintest clue why, except that her eyes seemed to look directly into his soul.

But all of that was ancient history now.

Still, as he continued to wait, he had mixed feelings about how easily he'd been drawn back into her life.

He and Lisa had had little contact in the years since their breakup. He'd met Sara on a blind date and started a relationship in which he'd confused caring with love. When Sara had told him that she was pregnant, he'd married her, but they'd both realized quickly it was a mistake. The marriage had ended a short time later by mutual agreement. A year ago he'd made another impetuous decision, leaving the police force and joining what had turned out to be a financially beleaguered private investigation firm. The company was solely under his name now, and he was starting to get it back on its feet—but only just.

While Lisa was living her life to a precise formula, he'd been making rash and ultimately misguided decisions. Not that his son was a mistake in any sense of the word. His love for Peter was the reason he'd been rethinking his own life, even before tackling this case. His love for Peter had opened his eyes to the dangers of being a police officer, and his hours didn't provide the kind of flexibility he needed to be the kind of father he wanted to be. Although he was passionate about his job, being there for Peter was more important.

The day Sara had told him about the talent agent coming to her concert he had been shocked and unprepared for the rush of emotion, especially the fear that he might lose his son. How would he ever manage without Peter? How would Peter adjust to leaving his family—grandparents, uncles, aunts, cousins?

He couldn't see himself in L.A., and he didn't feel it was a place to raise Peter. But if he *didn't* move near Sara, his time with Peter would be made up of short visits and lots of travel. Sara and he had joint custody, which worked well for both of them and provided Peter with as much stability as possible. He couldn't imagine being without Peter, the everyday contact, the love that overwhelmed him whenever his son smiled.

He wanted to be an involved father, and that meant living close to his son.

Should he consider going to L.A.? It wasn't *his* idea of paradise, but did he have a choice?

His parents would be devastated. Peter spent many happy hours visiting his grandparents and playing with his cousins.

Thinking about his son reminded him of Lisa and what she was going through. Considering how important today was for Lisa, he'd told her his being here was for old times' sake, and that was part of it.

Only seeing her in Tank's office and again today, he felt the old attraction drawing him into her life, reminding him how good their love had been. No other woman had made him want to be near her every moment the way Lisa had. Lisa's welcoming arms made everything seem right.

Yet in a fit of anger and wounded pride, he'd hurt

her that night in the restaurant. He'd walked out and never tried to make amends. What an idiot he'd been!

He realized how hard it must have been for her that day in Tank's office. She'd just learned about her birth mother, and then was forced to accept the help of a man who had been responsible for so much pain in her life. And still, despite all of their history and their differences, she'd graciously accepted his assistance.

A rustling sound made him turn. Lisa came toward him, her face tense, her shoulders hunched against some unseen force.

"Would a friendly shoulder be in order?" he asked, searching her face for the source of her agony.

"A shoulder would be nice," she said, a catch in her voice.

He held out his arms, and she stepped into them as if she'd never stopped doing it.

"I met her. I met my mother," she said, her body trembling.

He cradled her gently. "What's she like?"

"She's been in a wheelchair for years. She's so frail and alone, so in need of care and attention," she whispered.

He glanced down at her. "Is that your nursing assessment?" he asked.

"Yeah, partly." She gave him the faintest of smiles. "But, Mason, she's had such a hard life, so many things have gone wrong for her, things she couldn't control. I can't imagine how it would feel to give up a child...to fear the future. All these years my mother loved me enough to offer me a better life, to put me first."

"But you've found her now. You can make a difference."

Her arms tightened around him. "Yes, and I've got plans for Mom—I want her to come live with me. There's so much I can do for her if I bring her to Durham. She needs an aggressive physiotherapy program, and I can organize and oversee that better if she lives there. And on top of that, I have a sister... finally, and she needs me. I have a sister. It doesn't seem possible."

Surprised and pleased for her, Mason was glad he'd been here when she'd found her family. "Lisa, that's wonderful. You've waited so long to find your mother, and now a sister. How different your life will be from here on."

"Yeah, it *is* wonderful, and strange at the same time."

They stood there in the hallway holding each other the way they used to, and Mason was acutely aware of how right it felt to him.

She must have felt it, too, because the old Lisa reasserted herself. Suddenly she pulled out of his arms. Tucking long strands of her blond hair behind her ears, she fixed him with an anxious look.

"My sister's name is Anne Marie Lewis. She's five years older than me. It's so strange…to be needed, to be the one who can truly change someone's future. All my life my parents pampered me and loved me while my own family was left to struggle with so much less. If only I'd known… I've got to find Anne Marie. She's in trouble."

Mason recognized that look of exhaustion in Lisa's eyes. He'd seen it many times when he'd arrive at her apartment after her evening shift in Emergency. Lisa was feeling stressed, and who wouldn't be after what she'd been through?

"Why don't we get you checked in and something to eat first, and then you can tell me about your mother and your sister."

AN HOUR LATER, Lisa followed Mason down the hotel corridor without paying much attention to her surroundings. On the drive here from the nursing home, all she could think about were her mother's parting words.

How could Anne Marie have ended up in jail? Her mother hadn't said any more, and Lisa had been too shocked to ask. Afraid she couldn't cope with the situation, she'd practically run from the room.

Yet those few minutes with her mother had changed her life forever.

She had finally met the woman who gave birth to her. The one person who could tell her who she was, where she came from. Although she'd been nervous about meeting her mother, her fears had all been washed away in those first moments with Carolyn Lewis.

Instead of a woman with a dark secret as she'd feared, her mother was a woman who'd had the strength to survive in the face of difficulties that would have discouraged and demoralized a lesser person.

And now after years of wondering, Lisa would have a chance to learn all about her family. In the meantime, her mother and her sister needed her, and she'd be there for them.

She'd never had to take charge of a family situation before. But her family was desperate for help, and she was the only one who could provide it.

These feelings were as foreign as the world she found herself in—her mother unable to care for herself, her sister in jail.

As they arrived at the room Mason had booked for her, he opened the door, then put her suitcase down inside. He gave her a quick, assessing glance.

She couldn't meet his eyes because she couldn't let him in on what she was planning. If she did, he'd be determined to give her advice, make his opinions known. But tonight she could only deal with her own feelings. Now that she'd found her family, one thing was clear. She would help them, whatever it took.

"What's running through your head?" he asked.

"What do you mean?" she responded, feeling guilty for ignoring Mason since they'd left the nursing home. She'd spent her time in the car staring out the window, her heart in turmoil.

She hadn't told Mason very much about her visit with Carolyn. He hadn't pushed her for more, although she knew the cop in him wanted to ask.

"Look at me."

Lisa was vaguely aware of the old attraction stirring between them as their eyes met. The rise and fall of his chest as he held her gaze told her he felt it, too.

"I'm going to order dinner for us. Fried chicken, Caesar salad and baked potato for you."

She was grateful, not only that he remembered her favorite meal, but that he was willing to assume responsibility for her comfort.

Yet she dared not say that to him. Doing so would bring back old memories of better times.

She couldn't let herself think of what might have been. Finding her mother had already filled her with regret. All the moments they'd missed, moments of being together, sharing their lives. "That's so kind of you."

"What are friends for?" He grinned the familiar grin she remembered so well.

"You should have a hot bath, something to eat and go to bed before you fall asleep standing up."

"Sounds heavenly, but I have to make a call first."

"Why?"

"There's something I haven't told you about my sister... She's in jail," Lisa said, sitting down on the edge of the bed, her energy suddenly spent and her mind weary with everything she'd seen and heard in the past hours.

"What has she been charged with?"

"I have no idea. Sorry for springing this on you, but so much has changed."

He knelt down in front of Lisa, taking her hands in his warm grip, his smile uneasy. His touch brought forward long-buried memories of other times he'd knelt like this, his eyes filled with desire.

Resisting the urge to follow the memories, her body tensed.

"Which jail?" he asked, his voice calm and reassuring.

Oh, how she needed his calm approach! "I have no idea."

"But you'd like to see her while you're here."

"Yes, as soon as possible."

"You'll have to wait until tomorrow at the earliest."

She nodded. "I'll feel much better once I've talked to her," she murmured.

"Maybe. Maybe not. But I'll make some inquiries first thing in the morning...try to determine where she is and if you can visit her," he said, his doubtful tone raising her determination.

He clearly didn't understand her feeling of urgency, but if he was going to help her, she had to make him understand.

"Mason, you've known all along how my parents behaved when I asked about my biological family. Every time I'd ask questions, I'd end up wishing I hadn't."

"Maybe they had good reasons. Think about it. Your parents were kind people who loved you."

"And I didn't have the courage to insist that I be allowed to look into my past. I let my parents keep me from my family all those years when I could've gotten to know them. And even as an adult, I didn't go looking for any of my birth family. It was a mistake, and I have to take full responsibility for not searching. I want…no, I *need* to do everything I can for them."

"Lisa, I can see how this has affected you, but don't make any decisions right now. You've had a long drive and an emotionally exhausting experience. You should get a handle on the situation before you do anything."

"My sister's in jail. What other information do I need?"

"You're not listening," he said, his voice edgy. "You don't have any knowledge of Anne Marie Lewis or her past. What if she's a hardened criminal? What if she doesn't want to meet you? What if seeing her puts you at risk—"

"After all the times you accused me of not being a risk-taker, now you're telling me that visiting my sister could be dangerous. What right—"

"Lisa, let's not bring our past into this."

"How can I not? Our past is always between us," she responded, wishing she could ease the anxiety roaring through her.

But his question had made her wonder. Was she actually ready to visit her sister in jail? One minute she was and the next she wasn't.

"Well, we can't do anything about it at this hour," he said, glancing at his watch as he stood. He started for the door, stopped and turned back. "Do you want me to order food now, or what?"

She wanted him to hold her the way he'd done at the nursing home. She wanted to feel safe and secure. Sure in the belief that all of this would work out for the best.

Was she hoping for the impossible? Maybe. "Would you do me a favor? Could you try to find out tonight where she is and when I can see her?"

"Even if she's in the local jail, it's unlikely you could get in on such short notice. That is, if she's willing to see you," he muttered.

Lisa took a deep breath to ease the tension snapping through her and felt the flush of exhaustion as it laid claim to her limbs.

As much as she hated to admit it, Mason had a point—at least about the timing—but she refused to consider that Anne Marie might not want to see her. "I'd call myself if I thought they'd listen to me." She gave him a weary smile. "They'll listen to you, though."

His expression relaxed as he tapped his fingers on the door. "I'll order our food, make a couple of inquiries. I'll be back here as soon as I can," he said, opening the door.

"Mason, thank you for everything."

"Including the argument?"

"Yes," she sighed, relieved to see a real smile on his face.

"I'll be back," he said, closing the door behind him as he left.

Even with Mason gone from the room, his scent lingered, sparking memories of their first trip to New York and the carriage ride through Central Park, his arm protectively around her shoulders as the carriage moved beneath the canopy provided by the trees, the kiss they shared as the driver snapped their picture. She had kept that photo to remind her of that unforgettable evening.

He was her first love, and she'd been totally infatuated. After their breakup, she'd dated the new pediatric oncologist at the hospital, which was a disaster.

Since then, she'd concentrated on her career and developing her skills as a pediatric nurse.

Anything but face the very real possibility that she might never get another chance to put things right with Mason—whether that meant getting back together or becoming friends. Either way, she was at least partly responsible for how their relationship had ended.

A COUPLE OF HOURS later after several phone calls—including one to Peter to say goodnight—Mason sat across from Lisa at the tiny table in her room. The sky outside blazed with the golden pink of the setting sun.

Mason noted Lisa's excited behavior, her animated conversation, her plans for moving her mother to Durham, and all the while he was relieved that she hadn't asked about his phone call to the Indian River jail.

Worried about what he had to tell her, he'd decided not to say a word unless she brought it up.

Lisa could be very stubborn, and for his money, she was on a wild-goose chase, but he didn't want her to get hurt. He hadn't had much opportunity to show how sorry he was for walking out on her—thanks to the way his life and hers had split apart—but he wished he could redo parts of his past.

Sitting so close—the scent of her reaching out to him—triggered an expectation… Of what, he wasn't certain.

Lisa's movements, the way she smothered her

baked potato in sour cream, the way she chewed every bite attentively and placed her napkin so neatly beside her plate when she finished were all familiar.

Funny how they were so compatible in their everyday lives, but when it came to the big decisions they had little in common.

Carefully placing her fork and knife on the plate, she rose and set it back on the room-service trolley. "So, what about my sister?" she finally asked, returning to her seat.

He sighed. "Anne Marie is in the Indian River jail. It's not far from here."

"Has she been charged?"

He attempted to keep his tone neutral. "I've arranged an appointment for ten-thirty tomorrow. You can ask Anne Marie then."

He'd had to pull a few strings to get Lisa in to see her sister. The prisoner usually decided who visited, but the officer had put Lisa's name on the list at his insistence. It seemed that Anne Marie Lewis had been uncooperative so far, which didn't bode well for tomorrow.

"What am I going to do when I go in there?" Lisa asked, her voice uneasy, her eyes dark.

What was she asking? Did she expect to be able to walk into the jail and take Anne Marie home? "You're going to meet her, maybe arrange to visit her again the following day."

"I don't mean *that*." She began to pace the narrow

room. "I mean, what am I going to say to her? How do I explain who I am? We're complete strangers. How do I begin the conversation? Hello, my name is Lisa and I'm your long-lost sister?" She suddenly spun around, a triumphant smile on her face. "I'll start with the photo of her and me."

"What photo?"

"Oh, I forgot to tell you. Carolyn—I mean, my mother—had a photo of Anne Marie and me taken in Myrtle Beach when I was eight. Oh, Mason, you're not going to believe this..."

As she told him the story, her expression held such joy and hope that Mason felt his heart grow heavy. In all the time he'd known Lisa, he'd never seen her so animated, so happy. Her eagerness to take action pleased him; yet a part of him wished *he* could have made her this happy.

Beyond any doubt, Lisa Clarke had been waiting for this moment of connection with her birth family. If only he'd realized how important it was to her, back when their love had been an unbreakable tie between them.

"Lisa, let's not rush this. You don't know any of the circumstances of your sister's case, but I've seen—"

"So many cases like this, right? People in jail."

"Yeah, I have."

"Mason, you still haven't told me why Anne Marie's there."

Damn! He didn't want to tell her, because the implications were too painful. But her tone of voice told him she wouldn't be put off. "Drug trafficking."

She stopped pacing. "Oh. No." Color drained from her face. "Not that. She couldn't be mixed up in drugs."

Mason saw the fear in her eyes and knew what had put it there. "This isn't like your father's case." He hoped that was the truth, but there was no way of being certain of anything at this point.

"I'm sure it's not," she said firmly.

Her father had nearly died when a drug trafficker decided to settle the score when Jim Clarke won the case against him. Jim Clarke had been shot getting into his car outside the Durham courthouse. When the hospital called Mrs. Clarke, she'd come to the school to pick up Lisa. On the way to the hospital, her mother had been driving so erratically that the police had stopped her and had to drive her the rest of the way. The next few weeks had been incredibly stressful and emotional for Lisa. Her father held on by a thread and her mother had been a hysterical wreck. Eventually her father had recovered, but he had retired from the D.A.'s office and become a stockbroker—a less dangerous occupation.

That was one of the few events in her past she'd been willing to talk about, which told him just how much of an effect it had had on her life.

"Do you want me to go with you to the jail?"

The dark fear in her eyes changed to relief. "That would be wonderful," she said, her voice warm. "Thank you."

"Lisa, you have to realize that you may not be able to help Anne Marie. The D.A. wouldn't hold her without evidence."

"I have to do what I can. Anne Marie is part of my family," she said, the deep circles under her eyes intensifying the starkness of her gaze.

Lisa had been the only woman in his life who could make him jump through hoops in his eagerness to please her. And here he was, years later, and he still wanted to jump.

He fought the urge to crush her to him, to comfort her, but that was a bad idea. They weren't lovers anymore, and his life was already complicated enough. "Lisa, this is all new for you," he said.

"Yeah, new and a little scary."

"Of course you want to be there for your mother and sister. But for now, you need to get some rest."

"I don't think I can sleep," she said.

She was standing there, still wearing the blue tank top and jeans she'd arrived in, looking so achingly vulnerable, he was in danger of risking what little relationship they still had at this point by letting his eyes meet hers.

"Why don't you lie down? I'll sit in the chair for a while and maybe you'll be able to sleep," he suggested, tucking his hands into the pockets of his jeans, his insurance against touching her.

"You're probably right," she said. Kicking off her shoes, she climbed onto the bed and pulled the comforter over her, while he folded his long frame into the most uncomfortable chair he could ever have imagined—all plastic and metal. There was no chance he'd fall asleep, he mused, his gaze traveling over Lisa's form in the room's half-light.

Despite what she'd been through in the past hours, she smiled as she closed her eyes. Odd as it seemed now, regardless of the disastrous end of their relationship and his misguided marriage, Lisa held a very special place in his heart.

But once this trip was over, Lisa would have a whole new life that revolved around her mother and sister. Lisa would do what was best for her new family, leaving him on the outside once again.

Her shuddering sigh forced his attention to her face. The tears glistening on her cheeks made him wish he could take her in his arms and hold her while she cried. He waited to see if she'd open her eyes and search for him.

She didn't. Instead, she turned away and settled down again as if he wasn't there. He continued to wait expectantly until he heard the deep, rhythmic breathing that told him she was asleep.

Feelings of emptiness created by her turning away assailed him. Even in her moment of need, she couldn't reach out to him. Had he accepted this job in the hope that he and Lisa might get back together?

In the quiet of the room, he knew the truth. He'd hurt the one woman he'd ever loved in such a way that neither he nor Lisa could forget it. If he'd had the courage that night to go back and apologize, there might have been a chance for them.

If only...

WHEN LISA WOKE the next morning, she couldn't believe she'd slept in her clothes. She'd never done that in her life! She glanced around, realizing that Mason had removed the empty dishes, closed the drapes and turned off the lights, a level of thoughtfulness she didn't remember him displaying before. Maybe being a dad had changed him.

Although tired from the excitement of meeting her mother, a strange elation tempered by uncertainty made her restless. She stretched, letting the knowledge that she had a mother and a sister seep through her.

When she'd fallen asleep, her mind had been focused on the charges against Anne Marie, and how difficult it was to believe that drugs were once again threatening to ruin the life of someone important to her.

She'd never forget the day her mother got the call. Her father had been shot and was undergoing emergency heart surgery. When they got to the hospital,

Alice Clarke's hysteria had forced the doctors to sedate her, leaving thirteen-year-old Lisa to wait alone for the surgeon to come and tell her that her father had survived the operation.

But oddly enough, it was during those long hours of waiting that she began to feel at home in the hospital, somehow part of the activity going on around her. She'd decided then that she wanted to go into nursing.

Her decision had been one positive thing to come out of that nightmare, and she felt hopeful about this situation, too. Because of her tiredness last night, Anne Marie's dilemma had appeared overwhelming. In the light of a new day there were possibilities she wanted to explore.

Energized, she called Mason's room and they made plans for going to the jail. Driving south of Melbourne toward Vero Beach, Lisa focused on Mason's very capable hands as they rested on the steering wheel—the same hands that had massaged her scalp after a long night shift in Emergency.

Don't think about that!

Pulling her thoughts away from his hands, she focused on the slight frown between his eyes as he kept his attention on the road. They hadn't talked very much at breakfast, mostly because Mason had seemed preoccupied.

"Thank you for last night," she said, trying to draw him into a conversation.

"You're welcome."

A tiny surge of trepidation made her choose her words carefully. "Mason, I want your advice."

He glanced at his rearview mirror before pulling out to pass a truck. "Sure. Fire away."

"I doubt Anne Marie has much money, and I have no idea whether she's got a lawyer. If she doesn't, I'm going to hire one for her. What do you think?"

His gaze pinned her. "Lisa, don't be too quick to get involved here. Talk to her first and then decide. There may be nothing you can do for Anne Marie, or you may discover that she's not interested in your offer."

"But I'm *already* involved. She's my sister! I'll do whatever I can for her," she said, feeling frustrated that he'd think her sister was someone to be avoided.

"And it's very kind of you to want to solve her problem for her." His voice seemed flat, somewhat disinterested, certainly without the enthusiasm she'd counted on.

Why had she harbored the notion that Mason would be on her side in this? Maybe because she'd been accustomed to him taking her side...

But that was the past. He was here to do a job, get paid and go back to his P.I. business. He'd made that clear in Tank's office.

"We're here," Mason said, turning into the parking lot of the jail.

Suddenly all her determination was swept away by the reality of this forbidding place. She swallowed over the lump pressing against her throat. "Will you come in with me?"

"If you want, but I'm not allowed to go into the visitors' room with you." He shut off the ignition, and in the ensuing silence, her courage seemed to drain away.

They went through the door and walked to the desk. Lisa listened in dread as Mason did all the talking. She signed a sheet with the necessary information, glanced one last time at Mason and followed a man dressed in a taupe uniform.

"Your conversation will be through video link," he explained when they'd stepped into a small room.

"Video link? You mean I can't meet her in person?"

"For security reasons, the prisoners are in another building. You'll be able to talk to Anne Marie Lewis and see her on the monitor. It's close enough for you to see her well. You have thirty minutes, ma'am," the officer said, his smile bleak.

Sinking into the cold plastic of the chair, she stared at the video screen. In the silence of the airless room, she ran through what she wanted to say to her sister, the strain of the past few days filling her with misgivings. She'd only been sitting there a couple of minutes when a tall woman with brown hair, dark-framed glasses and prison garb appeared. Lisa's stomach knotted.

The fluorescent lighting emphasized her dull, limp hair and sallow skin. Anne Marie didn't look much like the girl in the photo.

"Who are you?" Anne Marie demanded. "I didn't ask for a visit with you." Her eyes radiated distrust, the hard rasp of her voice adding force to her words.

Lisa was so disappointed she could hardly say what she'd rehearsed on the way over here. "Hi, ah, I'm Lisa Clarke, and I'm your sister."

"My sister. I don't have a sister." Anne Marie's brown eyes glared at the camera. "Where's the proof that you're my sister?" she asked, sitting back in the narrow chair and crossing her arms over her chest.

The lack of emotion in Anne Marie's voice stunned Lisa. She'd expected her sister to be as excited as she was. Was Mason right? Was this woman beyond caring that she had a sibling?

"Anne Marie, I realize this is a bit of a shock for you. It's a long story. My adoptive mother died, and she left a letter revealing that my birth mother was alive. I hired a private investigator and he found Carolyn Lewis. She told me about you. I was with your...our mother yesterday and I saw the photo of you in her room."

"The photo?"

"Yeah, the picture of you and me in Myrtle Beach."

"Don't try to con me. The kid in that photo was you? *And* you're my sister? You're lying. Mom would've said if she'd known that was you. Why would she keep a secret like that?"

"I'm not sure. But I can tell you I had the best time that day on the beach, and you were so good to me. Remember the sand castle we made and those two boys who knocked it down? Remember how you chased them up the beach?"

Anne Marie leaned toward the monitor, placing her hands flat on the table. "Look, I don't know what you're after, but there's no way my mother would've hidden that kind of thing from me. We're close. Real close."

"Well, join the club. My adoptive parents kept our mom a secret from *me*."

"You mean you really didn't know about your own mother?"

Lisa nodded.

Anne Marie pursed her lips. "Okay, if you are who you say you are, what did I tell you I wanted to be?"

"An astronaut. You'd been to the Kennedy Space Center and you—"

The video screen caught the sudden sheen of tears in Anne Marie's eyes. "Lisa. And you're really my little sister?"

"Yes. When I visited Mom yesterday, she talked about you and about how difficult life has been, how much she wanted to keep us together, but couldn't."

"Yeah, you escaped while I had to make it on my own. Why didn't you come before?"

"I only just found out about you yesterday. When I learned you were in jail I had to come and see you."

"It'll be hard to get to know one another with me in here." Anne Marie shrugged.

"I'm willing to give it a try if you are. I'm so happy I found you."

Anne Marie glanced at the monitor, her hands clenched on the table as her expression ran the gamut from studied indifference to relief and caring. "Me, too."

Lisa reached across the empty space, smiling in relief at her sister's words.

Anne Marie pushed her glasses up on the bridge of her nose. "Sorry for being nasty, but I thought you were someone looking to make trouble for me. When they said I had an unscheduled visitor, I never imagined it would be you." Anne Marie moved closer, her face almost filling the screen. "I had no idea I had a sister, but I'm so glad you're here. My life is such a mess—" A gulping sob escaped her lips. She covered her face with her hands; her thin shoulders began to shake.

"Oh, Anne Marie, please don't cry. I'm here. We'll

have lots of time to get to know each other, just as soon as you're out of here."

Anne Marie raised her head, her expression devoid of hope. "It won't happen. I'm in on drug-trafficking charges. I'm innocent, but no one believes me."

"I do," Lisa said impulsively. She *had* to believe in her sister. Anne Marie deserved her family's support. Yet the shock of the past days made her hands tremble. She hid them in her lap and stared across the room at Anne Marie's image.

"Do you have a lawyer?"

"Not that you could tell by what's been going on. Jeff keeps urging me to be patient, but he never comes to see me."

"Who's Jeff?"

"Jeff Wallace. He's—he *was* my boyfriend, but I'm not sure what he is anymore. I think he may have framed me. I've never been in trouble with the law, and now this." Anne Marie grimaced and looked away from the screen.

Lisa had urgent questions about how her sister had ended up here, but it wouldn't be long before the officer returned. "Anne Marie, I want to help you and Mom. I'm going to take Mom back to Durham with me."

"You'd do that?" Anne Marie's expression brightened.

"She's our mother, and I want her to have the best."

"Thank you so much. I was trying to figure out how I could make the payment for her place in the nursing home while I'm locked up. She's been getting some money from the government but it's not enough. I've been worrying about Mom…and so many other things."

"Well, you can cross Mom off your list. As for you, a good lawyer will get these charges dropped," Lisa said emphatically, feeling optimistic for the first time since she'd entered the room.

"But, Lisa, the evidence they have against me is frightening. My name's on the deed as owner of a house where drugs were sold. I can hardly believe this is happening to me. They claim to have video surveillance of me meeting with local dealers. All I ever met with were my friends or Jeff's."

"I don't care what they have. You're entitled to a good defense, and I've got the money to provide it."

"Where did you get it from?" Anne Marie asked, suddenly suspicious.

"My adoptive parents, the same ones who didn't tell me about you or my…my mom. It only makes sense that the money they left should be used to defend my family, don't you think?"

Anne Marie's quiet sobs rose over the speakers. "I…I can't believe you're here. I've prayed every day since this happened that someone would get me out of this mess."

"I'm here and I'm going to stay until I get Mom ready to move back with me. After I have her settled in my house, you can come to Durham if you want. Don't worry," Lisa said, prepared to do whatever it took to support her family. No one should have to live without hope, especially her own sister.

Anne Marie wiped her eyes, swallowed hard and stared across the video link at Lisa. "Are you serious?"

"Completely."

There was a long pause while Anne Marie looked at something above the monitor, then her gaze returned to the screen. "Lisa, I have a huge favor to ask."

"Name it," Lisa said, happy to see Anne Marie's willingness to trust her.

"I have a daughter. She just turned three. She's with a friend of mine right now, but she—my friend—can't keep her much longer." Anne Marie's lips trembled; her eyes swam with tears. "Katie's my life. I can't face prison knowing she could end up in some horrible foster home."

Oh. No. There was a child trapped in this nightmare? "Where's the father?"

"Jeff's not interested in Katie. I already asked him."

"You must have other friends who could look after her. Besides, with a decent lawyer, you'll be—"

"Would you bring her back to Durham with you and Mom?"

There was no way in the world she could take on the responsibility of a three-year-old. She wasn't capable of caring for a child; she'd proven that the night Linda Jean Bemrose nearly died thanks to her carelessness. Because she couldn't forgive herself for what she'd done, she'd spent her entire life away from children. Working as a pediatric nurse had been helping her cope with her anxiety around children, but she still fought it every day. She was the wrong person to be Katie's guardian.

"I don't— I mean, I'm not good with kids. Besides, you'll be out on bail. I've got the money—"

"Lisa, please understand. I really appreciate that you want to hire a lawyer for me, but it won't matter. I'm going to prison." She hid her face with her hands again, then shifted her gaze to the monitor.

"I can survive anything, anything at all, if Katie's safe. Katie's an easygoing little girl. She's your niece. You'll love her. Please," Anne Marie begged. "Please take care of Katie."

CHAPTER FOUR

LIKE A SLOW-MOVING freight train gaining momentum as the minutes ticked by, shock and dread rolled over Lisa.

She tried to form the words to deny her sister's plea.

The troubled look in Anne Marie's eyes made her feel guilty, but fear and children went together in Lisa's life. Her attempt to overcome her fears and guilt by working on pediatrics had gone well...so far.

But seeing how vulnerable sick children could be, how quickly their condition could change and how helpless she felt when things went wrong, all intensified her lack of self-confidence where children were concerned.

There was simply no way she could take on a toddler, even if she wanted to. She had no personal experience with kids that would guarantee Katie's safety and happiness. Working in a hospital with qualified staff was one thing. Being totally responsible for an innocent little girl twenty-four hours a day, seven days a week, was an entirely different situation.

"Anne Marie, Katie would be so much better off with someone who has kids she can play with."

"Katie's easy to care for. She sleeps through the night. She's been in day care three days a week for the past year, and she's toilet trained."

"But what am I supposed to *do* with her? I mean…I have a job, other demands."

"You said you're moving Mom back to Durham with you, and Katie would be so good for Mom. I haven't been able to take Katie to visit her grand-mother as often as I'd like. But if she was living in the same house, the three of you would be able to get to know one another. Mom would be thrilled."

"You don't understand. I've never looked after anything—not a child, a cat, a dog or even a goldfish. Katie's not safe with me—"

"Lisa, I had so many dreams, and I've made so many mistakes. I didn't start out this way. Mom loved me and Aunt Helen was good to me, but I never had anything or anyone to call my own—until Katie. I quit school, and that was a big mistake, but I needed to work. Hooking up with Jeff was another mistake— except for Katie. If you'll help me just this once, I promise you the minute I'm free I'll come and get her."

Lisa continued to listen to Anne Marie across the video link, her mind in complete turmoil. She realized what a pampered child she'd been, free of any problems or worries. Sure, her parents had kept secrets from her, and her mother had planted all these fearful ideas about kids, but she'd always known love and security—maybe too much security.

To be trapped in jail, waiting for whatever justice there'd be and fearing that your daughter wouldn't be well cared for, had to be terrifying. Lisa rubbed her hands to ward off a sense of the inevitable.

What if she didn't take Katie? Where would the girl end up? Was this how it'd been for her mother all those years ago when she'd given *her* up for adoption? Or had it been much worse? How would it feel to give up a child you loved because you couldn't provide for her?

She'd confronted her mother with her anger over being abandoned. Yet wasn't she doing the same thing to her niece if she refused to take her? Katie deserved to be with relatives, especially considering her mother's situation. Whatever happened in Anne Marie's life, Katie needed to be cherished by her family.

She had a home for Katie, and Anne Marie was right about their mother. She'd be overjoyed to be with her granddaughter in Durham.

Still, it was such a big decision. "I'll think about it—"

The door whooshed open behind her. "Ma'am, your time is up."

"Please, Lisa, say you'll do it. I'll sign anything to have her safe with you."

So often, Lisa had imagined having a family of her own, sharing everything with her sister or brother—but never like this. "Anne Marie, I can't."

"I'll give you Cindy's phone number. Lisa, go and see Katie. Judge for yourself what a wonderful little girl she is," she added quickly.

Despite the cool indifference of the monitor, Lisa could see the stark look in Anne Marie's eyes. If she didn't help her sister now, there wouldn't be a second chance. What had her dad once said to her? Some moments only happen once in a lifetime.

This is what you've always wanted—a family to care for, someone who shares your blood, who knows who you were and where you came from. What are you waiting for?

"Ma'am?"

Lisa motioned to the officer. "One minute, please."

She turned back to the video link, meeting the anguished expression on her sister's face. Feeling her heart open up to the plea she saw in her sister's eyes, she said, "I'll take Katie…for now. Mom and I will look after her. And I promise, I'm going to get you out of here so you and Katie can be together. Katie should be with her mother."

"I'm so glad you're my sister, Lisa. You won't regret this, I promise."

The trust in Anne Marie's eyes fanned hope in Lisa's heart. Her sister and her niece needed her, and being needed was something entirely new. Suddenly she felt strong, decisive and in control.

She'd get her mother to help her with Katie, and she'd talk to her friends at work about how to care for a toddler. She was a nurse with experience in pediatrics. This could work. Besides, it would only be for a little while. "I'll go and get my niece."

As her words floated across the room her heart tripped in her chest, sending anticipation spreading through her.

"And I'll make sure you get a proper lawyer."

"I'll pay you back. I'll make this up to you."

Lisa responded to the wholehearted smile on Anne Marie's face with a reassuring one of her own. "That's not necessary. I'll do the best I can with Katie…and Mom. We're family, and family sticks together."

IMPATIENT, MASON LEANED against the car as he listened to the potential client on his cell. Tank had referred a woman to him who suspected that her husband was cheating on her, and she had the money to pay his investigation fees.

He wanted to refuse the job. Marital issues and surveillance might be a P.I.'s bread and butter, but that was all you could say for it as far as he was concerned. The money was good, though, and he needed to build a solid track record with Tank, who had the connections to get him more interesting, high-profile cases. And building the business was his number-one priority.

He held the phone to his ear, trying to offer suggestions while he kept a lookout for Lisa. She'd been in the jail for over half an hour and he was becoming more concerned with each passing minute. True, there was no way for Anne Marie Lewis to do her any physical harm, but Mason worried more about the psychological impact of this particular reunion.

He'd had the impression from the officer that Anne Marie had no financial or emotional support, a difficult situation for anyone. Lisa's need to connect with her birth family made her a perfect target for an unscrupulous person.

Finally, his new client seemed satisfied and hired him on his promise that he'd meet with her within forty-eight hours. He was confident that he could head back to Durham just as soon as Lisa had made plans to move her mother there. In the meantime, he'd get his assistant, Tim Harris, to organize surveillance for the new client.

Suddenly Lisa was walking across the parking lot toward him, a shocked look on her face. Damn! What had happened?

He slipped his cell phone into the case on his belt and jammed his fists into the pockets of his jeans, his good old-fashioned guarantee against touching her. "How'd it go?"

"Anne Marie and I talked," she said, squinting

into the sun, seemingly unaware that her sunglasses were perched on her head.

She was chewing her lower lip, which told him her stress level was pretty high. "That's great."

She adjusted her purse strap on her shoulder, resting the other hand on her hip. "She's agreed to allow me to hire her a lawyer, and I'm going to have to stay here longer than I planned."

Mason glanced around the parking lot, resisting the urge to slide back into the old habit of taking her hand and playing with her fingers. "Why, is there a problem?"

"She has a daughter, a little girl named Katie."

He wasn't completely surprised by this development. He'd seen it many times in his police work. A woman without the money to train for a career very often hooked up with a man who could support her. Unfortunately, the situation was frequently worsened by the addition of children.

"A little girl. How do you feel about that?" he asked, knowing Lisa's response all too well. No wonder she was chewing her lip. The dream of finding her family had not included a niece.

"I'm an aunt, and it's... I guess it's different. I never expected to be an aunt."

Given that she'd babysat only once in her entire life—an upsetting experience, as he recalled—he doubted she'd be willing to do it now. "I assume you plan to meet Katie."

Lisa looked him straight in the eye, making it impossible for him to miss the hope in her expression. "No, it's a lot more than that. I'm bringing Katie home with me...and Mom."

"Are you crazy? You're going to take Katie?" What kind of game was this Anne Marie Lewis playing? "Lisa, don't be conned into assuming this woman's problems."

"I'm not, but I can't abandon my niece." The glint of determination in her eyes told him she'd already made up her mind.

Lisa never made snap decisions like this, so there was only one possible explanation. Anne Marie Lewis had laid a guilt trip on her, and softhearted Lisa had fallen for it.

"You won't be abandoning her. You'll visit her, provide for her and you can even arrange a home for her in Melbourne, if you like. But taking Katie home with you..."

"Mason, I want to do this."

What a hell of a mess. Lisa wasn't thinking straight or she'd see just how insane this whole plan was. "May I remind you what you said to me when I suggested *we* consider having kids?"

She frowned at him. "It was a lot more than a suggestion. You gave me an ultimatum."

He didn't want to argue with her, but he had to press his point—for her sake. "You said you weren't comfortable having children, that they make you nervous. How does that fit with becoming an instant mom?"

"Mason, I can't explain it. But it's as if somehow everything's shifted. Seeing Anne Marie alone and in need of my help, having my mother and now my niece enter my life, getting the opportunity to connect with them—it's all made me feel alive. I've been waiting for this for so long. You've always had a big family, so you can't begin to understand what it's like."

"Anne Marie must be happy with your plan," Mason said ruefully.

"That's not fair! You've never met my sister," Lisa said, moving past him to the passenger side of the car. "I'm not talking to you about this. I'm going to make arrangements to bring my mother and niece to Durham. You have no business interfering."

Frustrated by the stupidity of the situation, he watched her open the door and throw herself down in the seat of his carefully restored Corvette. He usually rented a car for cases, but on this one he'd wanted the comfort of his own car.

"You can't help people who won't help themselves," he muttered, going to the driver's side of the car.

"What did you say?" she asked suspiciously.

Her frown of displeasure was the final straw. Lisa Clarke thought she knew what she was doing; as a result, his opinion didn't count. "Nothing."

He'd come here to find her mother, and he'd succeeded. She'd decided to take on the problems of her family, despite his advice to the contrary. But Lisa was right. He had no business interfering in her plans.

"What's your next step?" he said, fishing around in his pocket for the keys. He kept his voice calm and even.

They sat in the sweaty silence of the car, both staring out the window at the waves of heat coming off the asphalt.

Mason refused to start the engine until he'd made one last plea. "Lisa, you've got a full-time job that you're devoted to, you're moving your mother into your home and in the past couple of years you've lost both your parents. That's more than enough change for anyone."

Lisa continued to stare straight ahead. "Mason, I've got a chance to learn about my family and where I came from. Did I tell you I resemble my dad?"

Again, he saw the hope in her eyes, heard the certainty in her voice, and despite everything he wanted to touch her cheek. "No."

"He was handsome. My parents loved each other deeply. Mom lost the love of her life, and now she's found me, and I've found her."

How could he be angry with Lisa for doing what she did best—caring for people. "I just want you to be sure of what you're doing."

"Anne Marie has no one to look after her daughter while she's awaiting trial—"

"And if she gets out on bail? Will she come back for the girl then, or is she going to pursue her career in drug trafficking while you play mommy to her daughter?" he asked, more harshly than he'd intended.

"How dare you say that! You didn't see her. You have no idea what she's been through."

She couldn't be this naive. Did she really believe this woman's story? "Neither do you. You don't know how much of what she's telling you is the truth and how much is a fictional story to gain your support."

"May I remind you that I'm not the only person who makes snap decisions involving children?" she said.

"You're referring to Peter."

She nodded, her jaw set. "You and I broke up less than a year before you and Sara had a son, which proves just how determined you were to have kids."

Mason felt his cheeks flare red at her remark. "Lisa, leave our problems out of this."

"I will if you stop trying to make me do things your way. Mason, all I'm asking for is a chance to make things right for my family. You would do the same," she said stiffly.

LISA WAS SUFFOCATING from the heat, which increased her discomfort as she waited for Mason to respond. "Mason, don't be angry," she finally said. "Have a little faith in me and in Anne Marie."

Resting his arms on the steering wheel, he looked over at her. "It's not about having faith." He sighed. "Lisa, as your friend, I want you to think about this before you go ahead."

There was genuine concern in his voice—a friend's concern. And Mason, like her parents, had always offered her advice.

The difference was that now, with her parents gone, she'd begun to like feeling in charge of her life, making her own decisions. So far, those decisions had been relatively small ones.

She wished Mason could support what she was about to do, but he obviously couldn't. Yet she couldn't renege on her promise to Anne Marie.

"Mason, I realize you believe I'm making a huge mistake, but I've made up my mind. I'm going to take Katie and Mom back to Durham as soon as I possibly can."

MASON LEANED TOWARD her, wishing he could ease the distress in her eyes. Although her naiveté was downright frightening at times—thanks to her parents—there was nothing he could do to stop her. Nor could he reassure her. "It's your decision."

She moved closer to the door as tears welled in her eyes. "Mason, I thought you of all people would understand what I'm feeling. You love kids. Would you want a vulnerable three-year-old to be left in the care of complete strangers?"

He didn't want to think about the child, even if Lisa had a point. In fact, she'd made a lot of good points. And he realized that he could voice all the objections he wanted, but she was determined to help her family.

"You're right. Your niece deserves to have you in her life."

She glanced at him in surprise. "You're not going to argue with me? Does that mean you agree with my plans?"

As he met her questioning gaze, he caught himself wanting to exert his control over her situation. But in the past few minutes he'd seen that Lisa had changed. She wasn't going to meekly acquiesce to his opinions or advice, as she had always been happy to do before and he had come to expect. "No, I'm simply accepting the fact that it's your life, your decision."

"Well, finally, I'm being heard," she said, a gentleness in her tone that indicated that she was relieved.

So why had he let himself get mixed up with this woman again? And why did it still hurt to know that she'd move heaven and earth to look after her niece when she hadn't agreed to have his children?

He sighed. "Lisa, yesterday at this time you hadn't even met your mother, and finding your sister and your niece came as a total surprise. So much has changed for you in the past few hours. Just think about this before you make the commitment to take Katie."

"Mason, there isn't any other family member who can take Katie, who can provide for her. I can't leave her here... I'm willing to try anything if it will make a positive difference in Katie's life. And even if I may not be the best fill-in mother, I can't leave Katie here to face an uncertain future."

"If the future includes Anne Marie going to prison for years, are you prepared to raise a child alone?"

CHAPTER FIVE

IT HAD BEEN a silent ride back to the hotel. In her room Lisa gathered her belongings and made a few calls to arrange for her mother's release from the nursing home.

She'd phoned Carolyn to tell her of the plan to bring her and Katie back to Durham. Her mother was delighted. In fact, she wanted to come with Lisa when she picked Katie up from the babysitter.

Next, Lisa had called Cindy Sharp, Anne Marie's friend who was keeping Katie, and was relieved to hear real caring in her voice. She seemed concerned for Anne Marie's situation and for Katie's. They'd agreed to meet after lunch.

On her way out the door, she ran into Mason.

"You're leaving, I assume," he said, the coolness in his tone emphasizing the distance growing between them.

"I'm going to pick up Katie."

His eyes were dark, his gaze analytical. "Have it your way."

"I will," she said defensively. "I don't get it, Mason. Why are you so upset about me wanting to help Anne

Marie and Katie? You would've done the same for any of your sisters or brothers."

There was a long pause while he studied her, then shoved his hands through his hair before resting them on his hips. "You're right. I'd do anything for my family."

"There. You see? I'm only doing what you would do in the same circumstances."

"Lisa, being a parent, caring for a child, is not some sort of clinical trial where you look for results or change your plan when things don't work out. If you take Katie, you could very well end up raising her. What if your sister doesn't come back for her, and you find you can't cope with a child? What then? What kind of damage will you have done to your niece by rushing into this?"

His words slammed into her with such force she stepped back and sat down hard on the bed. What had made her think she could look after a little girl—and what would happen if Anne Marie went to prison?

Maybe Anne Marie's problems were partly due to growing up without a father and with a sick mother; in the same way, Katie might not have a father or a mother, only an aunt and an aging grandmother.

Lisa's nursing experience with children made her well aware of how critically important those early years were to the normal development of a child. Was she ready to be Katie's mother should Anne Marie go to prison? How would she cope with being a single parent?

She hated to admit it, but Mason had a point. She hadn't thought this through very well at all. She'd been so easily swayed by Anne Marie's pleading and her own need to reach out to her family.

What have I done?

What had made her agree to something this difficult? She couldn't do it—not now, not ever! If only she could retract her commitment to Anne Marie. Feeling faint, she forced air into her lungs, waiting for the fear and anxiety to run its course.

"Lisa, put your head between your knees," Mason said, a gentle tone in his voice. "Deep breaths."

She listened to his instructions, her mind searching for a way out of the situation. What should she do? She'd promised to pick up Katie. She wished she could count on Mason, the old Mason who'd loved her.

"Lisa, I didn't mean to be so hard on you." He took her hands in his as he knelt down. "You have to figure this out for yourself. What do you want to do?"

She hesitated, all her fears rising to the surface. Indecision plagued her every thought. "What do I want to do? I...I want to do what's best for Katie. She's an innocent child caught up in her mother's problems. Katie shouldn't have to be lonely or afraid."

"And you're willing to tackle the job of making

her world safe until her mother comes back?" he said, his voice a whisper, his breath on her cheek.

"I...I'll try."

"I'll help you, if you want."

She couldn't believe it. Had he read her thoughts, her hope that he would become involved? "You will?"

"Lisa, we may not be lovers, but we can still be friends."

The words jabbed at her heart. Despite her earlier regret that he'd made no effort to be her friend, somehow being friends seemed like the end of something, not the beginning. "Thank you. I really appreciate your kindness."

Relieved, and not wanting to do anything to jeopardize the closeness she was feeling as they sat together on the end of the bed, his hand touching hers, Lisa wished she could hold on to this moment.

Mason had to get back to Durham. But now she was reasonably confident that he'd be there when she got home, which was more than she'd expected from him. "What time do you think you'll get home?"

He sighed, rubbed his palms on his jeans. "I'm not leaving today."

Surprised, she glanced at him. "You're not?"

"I may not agree with what you're doing, but I understand why you're doing it. If you like, I'll talk to Tank about a good lawyer for Anne Marie. And

I'll ask if he can pull a few strings and get us in to see the lawyer today."

She attempted to clear her throat. "Sure. Yeah, that would be great."

His arm came around her, his body providing a haven. For a fleeting moment they were together. Oh, how she wished they were a couple, supporting each other, caring for each other. But they weren't and she had to remember that.

"Mason, I don't know what to say."

His arm tightened around her, his voice soft in her ear. "I owe you this."

Mason took charge of contacting the necessary people. She listened as he talked to Tank about a lawyer, an investigator, all the other details, and the tension began to ease from her body.

Mason was looking after her once again. And despite all her reservations to the contrary, it was exactly what she needed. At least for today.

LATER, LISA STILL hadn't figured out why Mason had changed his mind about staying, but she was delighted he had. Tank and Mason must have worked quickly, because they had an appointment with Ruben Watt, the lawyer, for two o'clock. Lisa was anxious to hear his opinion.

She called Cindy to tell her they'd be coming to get Katie later than she'd promised, then she phoned

Carolyn to bring her up to date. Her mother had insisted she come to the lawyer's office with her.

Lisa argued against it at first, but then realized that her mother had every right to be there. If it were *her* daughter's fate being discussed she'd want to be there, too.

Entering the nursing home she couldn't help noticing how different it was from the first time. Her mother sat in a wheelchair just inside the double doors. Lisa had bought a new folding wheelchair that would fit in her car, and with the help of a nurse, Lisa settled her mother in the front seat.

As they drove to Melbourne, Lisa and her mother chatted sporadically, the visit to Rubin Watt's office being the one subject they didn't touch upon.

When they reached the office, Mason was waiting, and took over wheeling Carolyn's chair as they went into the reception area.

Before they could settle in, Rubin Watt appeared. "Tank Tweedsdale and I went to law school together, but I preferred warm weather and ended up here," he said jovially as he beckoned them into his office.

Once seated and the introductions complete, he glanced at each of them in turn. "I know this is a very difficult situation for all of you, but it will get better, you'll see. I haven't had much time to go over Anne Marie's case, but I did talk to the D.A., and I spoke with Anne Marie. The D.A. feels they have a pretty solid case against her."

"No! That can't be!" Carolyn gasped, her fingers digging into the arms of the chair. "It's that man, that creep she lived with—he's the criminal, not my Anne Marie. Anne Marie wouldn't harm anyone. She'd never be involved in drugs. She's a good daughter and mother," she half shouted as tears began streaming down her cheeks.

Lisa reached over, taking her mother's trembling hand in hers. "Mom, please don't cry. It's going to be all right," she murmured over the sinking feeling that invaded her.

"Mrs. Lewis, we've all been touched in some way by drugs. And I believe that your daughter was probably the victim of circumstances, that the man she was living with graduated from possession to trafficking and Anne Marie was caught in the middle. I just have to prove it. And I will. I apologize for not being as familiar as I should be with the case, but time didn't allow me to read everything. But I promise you she will have good legal representation. You can depend on me."

"What did you find out about Jeff Wallace?" Mason asked, his voice reassuringly calm.

The lawyer riffled through his papers. "He's been picked up on possession of marijuana before. The police have had him under surveillance for some time. They've arrested him on trafficking charges."

"Is he talking?"

"Not yet. In the meantime, we'll get an investigator

on him..." Rubin Watt exchanged glances with Mason. "And see what he comes up with. What's important here is that you remain calm. Nothing's been decided. There's still a chance of finding something that'll get the charges dropped."

The only sound in the room was her mother's quiet sobbing.

"Mr. Watt, I want you to do everything in your power to clear my sister. She's innocent," Lisa said, trying to keep the desperation from her voice.

Not knowing where to turn, she looked at Mason. His eyes held hers and he smiled encouragingly. As they rose to leave the room, he came to her. "Lisa, I have to get back to Durham to deal with another case—will you be okay?"

His protective stance, the concern in his eyes, drew her to him. What she wouldn't give to have him put his arms around her, shield her from all the anxiety of the weeks ahead. Clutching her purse to stop herself from moving closer to him to seek out his strength, she said, "Yes, I'll be fine. I'm hoping to be on the road as soon as possible, anyway."

"Will you call me once you've left Melbourne?"

"Do you want me to?"

"I feel guilty about leaving you like this."

Mason feeling guilty? Having regrets? "You've been very kind, and despite my earlier misgivings, you've done more than I had a right to expect and I appreciate it."

"See you back in Durham?" he asked, squeezing her shoulder.

"Sure."

"Keep your cell phone on."

"I will." Lisa would keep it on because, despite everything, she didn't want to let him go.

THEY LEFT MASON at Rubin Watt's office while they headed over to the jail. Lisa wanted to visit Anne Marie before she went home, and so did Carolyn.

But as they pulled into the jail parking lot, her mother turned to her. "Do you think they'll let you talk to Anne Marie?" her mother asked, her eyes still damp from crying.

"Mason said he spoke with the people at the jail, and we can go in."

"I don't think I should. I hope you don't mind, but I can't let Anne Marie see me like this. It would only upset her more." Her voice shook. "You go, and give her my love. Tell her I'll write."

The jail procedure felt depressingly familiar as she sat in the chair in front of the monitor. When Anne Marie appeared she seemed smaller, her expression blank, as if the effort to show any emotion was too much.

"Anne Marie, your lawyer has started an investigation on your behalf. He seems very competent, and he'll have lots to tell us soon about your case," she said, her voice losing its force as she watched Anne Marie's listless behavior.

"All that matters is that you take Katie when you go back to Durham. Katie is all I care about," her sister said, staring despondently at the screen.

"Don't get discouraged, Anne Marie. You'll be free very soon," she said, anxious to see a hint of a smile on her sister's face.

"How can you be so sure?"

"Because...because you wouldn't be involved in anything that would hurt Katie."

Anne Marie grasped the edge of the table. "I would never, *ever* do anything to hurt Katie in any way. All I want is for you and Mom to give her all the love and attention she deserves. Whatever happens with me, please keep her safe."

"I promise," Lisa said, determination welling up in her.

AFTER GETTING HER mother packed up, Lisa took Carolyn over to Cindy Sharp's house to pick up Katie.

Her worry over whether she could cope with Katie had waned when she visited Anne Marie and saw her desperation. Whatever the outcome, she was committed to caring for her niece, in the firm belief that her sister would be free to come for Katie and resume her life.

Lisa couldn't back out now.

A sudden thought crossed her mind, making her smile. If Alice could see her now, she'd be swallowing pain pills and warning of an impending migraine.

Rounding the corner, she drove down into a cul-de-sac with double-wide trailers fanning out around the perimeter. She spotted number sixteen and parked at the curb. The driveway was littered with bicycles, basketballs, child-size lawn chairs and a huge toy dump truck. Tall grass covered what was left of the lawn.

Leaving her mother in the car, Lisa picked her way past the assortment of children's toys, and stepped up to the door leading to a screened-in porch. Her tap on the door was greeted by the wild barking of a dog, and a woman's voice ordering the dog to be quiet.

"Be right there," the same voice called from somewhere inside.

Lisa clasped her hands together to keep them from shaking while she waited what seemed like a lifetime for Cindy to appear.

"You must be Lisa. Anne Marie called a few minutes ago to talk to Katie. I look after children in my home—Anne Marie probably told you that—and Katie's one of my brightest. Come on in," she said, unlatching the screen door with one hand while she fended off a huge Burmese mountain dog who came charging toward the open door.

Lisa slipped inside, away from the dog, wondering

how she'd talk to her niece, her heart breaking at how the little girl must feel with her mommy gone, someone other than her mother taking care of her and a strange woman showing up at the door to meet her. "Is Katie here?"

"She sure is," Cindy said, closing the screen door and leading the way to the living room, dog in tow. "Katie, honey, come out and meet your aunt Lisa."

Before Lisa had time to think, a little girl with caramel-blond curly hair and pink cheeks ran into the living room, trailing a stuffed green dinosaur behind her. "Weesa?" the child asked, face turned up, an uncertain smile pulling at the corners of her mouth.

Lisa knelt down in front of her niece, her eyes searching for recognition—for connection. "Are you Katie?"

"Yes," the little girl sighed, her voice muffled by one hand reaching for her hair while she slipped the thumb of her other hand into her mouth.

"I'm Lisa. I'm your mommy's sister."

Huge dollops of tears rose in Katie's eyes, and her mouth twitched as the tears cruised down her cheeks.

Unable to bear the sight, Lisa scooped the child into her arms, her hands holding the tiny form close to her while soothing noises rose in her throat.

Katie's tears soaked Lisa's shirt as she sucked her thumb and snuggled into her arms. No one had ever clung to Lisa like this, no arms had revealed such dependency, and for a moment panic crept through her.

What if Katie continued to cry? What if she didn't like being with Lisa? What if the child got sick? She worked with the pediatricians at her hospital, but would she be any good at recognizing symptoms quickly?

She took a deep breath, remembering that her own family doctor had lots of experience with children. Hadn't she seen children in the waiting room whenever she had an appointment?

As she and Katie hugged each other, these worries and feelings of unease gave way to an overwhelming sense of connectedness. As the child's warmth met hers, compassion—mixed with a fierce need to protect this sweet little girl—made her unexpectedly thankful that Katie was part of her life now.

She held Katie gently as she soothed her with comforting words she hadn't ever used with another human being. Her arms trembled, not from the weight of the child, but from the emotional riptide pulling her into a close bond she'd never experienced before in her life.

Part of her wanted to hold on tight, to shield Katie from every bad thing in the world. Was this how it felt to love a child? To have this compulsion to protect a vulnerable little person from all and any upset or pain?

"Lisa, I realize this is a special moment for you and Katie, and I'm sorry to interrupt, but I have to get my day-care charges ready for their outing, and I have to drop my son Kyle off at soccer," Cindy said.

Still clutching Katie, Lisa stood and turned to Cindy. "I understand, and I must be going. I'm making arrangements to take Katie's grandmother home with me, as well."

"Anne Marie told me all about it, and I think what you're doing is wonderful. Anne Marie and her family are very lucky to have you."

"And I'm lucky to have them. But I won't keep you, so if you can help me gather Katie's things, I'll be on my way," Lisa said, refusing to let go of Katie. She'd carry her to the car, and get Cindy to help her put the car seat in.

"I'm afraid Katie doesn't have a lot to take. When Anne Marie was arrested, the social worker brought Katie to my house without anything. I went to her house, but the police were there looking for evidence and I couldn't get much." She shrugged.

"That's okay. I can buy whatever I need on the way home."

"Great," Cindy said, wiping her hands along the sides of her jeans. "I'll get her bag, and help you settle her in the car."

Katie lifted her head and stared after Cindy as she moved down the narrow hall, an anxious expression on her tiny features.

Urgently needing to put a smile on Katie's face, she said, "Katie, honey, why don't you and I go shopping? What do you say?"

Katie shifted her gaze to Lisa's face, her head tilted sideways, her eyes huge pools of uncertainty. "I want Nemo," she said, putting her thumb firmly in her mouth and burying her face back in Lisa's shoulder.

"Nemo, it is, then," Lisa said, while an unfamiliar happiness eased the tension between her shoulders.

CHAPTER SIX

ONCE LISA HAD finally gotten the car loaded, they were ready to get on the road. Lisa was thankful her car was big enough to hold everything, even though her mother and Katie had little to take with them and the wheelchair folded easily into the trunk. There had been so many things to do and arrangements to make that Lisa felt completely overwhelmed. She could have stayed another night in Melbourne, but she wanted to get back.

She had to sort out her feelings over all the changes taking place in her life; to do this she needed to be at home.

A few weeks ago, she hadn't known she had a family, and now, happy though she was, she sensed that her life was slipping out of control.

And then there was Mason. His sudden offer to go to the lawyer with her had been so welcome. Who would've believed that Mason could be such a good friend? Not her, for sure.

But even with Mason's help, she realized how poorly prepared she was to take on this much responsibility all at once.

Her mother had shown concern for how hard Lisa had worked to get everything organized, which Lisa appreciated, but it didn't change the sense of being in over her head.

It'll get better, she told herself as she pulled onto I-95. Lisa adjusted the rearview mirror so she could see Katie, who had been very quiet ever since they'd loaded the car.

What must Katie be thinking? Being put in a car with a stranger and without her mother would be frightening, to say the least. But the little girl's only response had been silence as she put her thumb in her mouth.

"We'll stop near Jacksonville tonight. I'll try for a motel with a pool so we can relax and cool off."

"That sounds wonderful," Carolyn said, with a huge smile and a look of complete pleasure warming her face. "It's so nice to be out of the nursing home. A mere week ago, I was pretty discouraged and worried about Anne Marie and Katie. And now I have so much to look forward to."

"We both have," Lisa replied, feeling the knot in her stomach ease.

"Lisa, you haven't told me how you found me."

"My mom died and left a note explaining that you were still alive, and my lawyer thought that you might still be in Florida."

"So, your mother finally did the right thing. It

must've been difficult for her to keep a secret like that for so long, but she obviously had her reasons."

"I can't imagine what they'd be."

"She was doing what she believed was best for you. As I did."

Lisa glanced across at her mother. "How can you be so...kind? If we'd met years ago, both our lives would have been different."

"Yes, darling, I'm sure they would have been, but regret will only bring sadness. Let's concentrate on the future. We have each other and, for now, we have Katie. And lots of happiness ahead for us."

Love and caring flowed from her mother's gaze, a love Lisa had never expected to experience. Yet her mother was right, the past was over, along with the waiting and wondering about who her parents were. "You're going to like being in Durham, Mom."

Her mother patted her shoulder. "I will. I can hardly wait to get there and see where you've lived all these years."

Despite her exhaustion, her mother's encouraging words filled her with purpose. Suddenly she wanted desperately to be in Durham and get her new family settled at the house.

She was relieved that she'd put off selling her parents' home—her family would need all the space in the big house. Since her mother liked the fact that she had a pool, she'd get the pool-service company to come as soon as possible and get it ready again.

Lisa's cell phone started to ring and she grabbed it. "Hello."

"How's it going?" Mason asked.

Mason's voice was a reassuring break from the emotional ebb and flow of the past few hours. "Fine so far. We're just north of Melbourne on I-95."

"So you'll make it to Jacksonville before you stop?"

"Hopefully."

"You've had a long day, and you've got an invalid and a child with you. I was hoping you'd wait until tomorrow to start back. I have to give you full marks for determination."

"Yeah, I was saved by my list-making skills," she responded, her grip on the wheel easing.

"I remember those infamous lists," he said, the sexy tone of his voice reverberating in her head. Somehow banter with Mason was easier when she couldn't see his face.

"How did you manage with Katie?"

Lisa glanced over her shoulder to find Katie asleep in her car seat. "Mason, she's adorable. And despite her anxiety when I picked her up earlier, she's adjusted so well. Of course, Mom helped," Lisa said, smiling across at her mother.

"You did it all, dear," her mother said, straightening her dress over her lap. "I only entertained Katie while you were busy."

"It sounds like your mother's a fan of yours already," Mason said.

"Yeah, and me of her," Lisa answered, feeling much better now that she was talking to someone who understood what an undertaking this was for her.

"I can't wait to get home. But we may be a couple of days on the road, since I've never traveled with a child before."

"All the more reason to take your time—and enjoy your family."

"That's what I was thinking. Maybe we'll stop in Myrtle Beach."

"Is there anything I can do here before you get home?"

She should tell him how much she appreciated the easy way he offered his help as if he'd been doing it all along. But having Mason around, accepting his help, was forcing her to think about what she wanted from him. She missed Mason's caring and support... and love.

Only, welcoming Mason back into her life meant coming to terms with how he had left her, how her trust in him had been damaged—maybe beyond repair—and opening herself up to that kind of pain again. Was the risk worth taking? She wasn't sure.

"I'm going to need a good carpenter. I have to make some changes around the house."

"You mean a wheelchair ramp?"

"Yes, and a few things inside, as well." She'd decided to convert her father's den into a suite for her mother so she'd be all on one level. "And I'll have to buy a crib. A stroller. I'm not sure what else."

"What? No list?" She could hear his smile.

"Not yet," she said, enjoying their moment together on the phone. So like other moments they'd shared when they were a couple.

"Don't worry about all that. I'll check with my sisters. One of them must have a spare crib kicking around, along with a whole bunch of toddler paraphernalia."

"That would be great."

"What are friends for?" he said, his voice gentle in her ear.

Friends. As emotionally draining as the past few weeks had been, it was good to know that she and Mason were finally friends.

Mason as a friend had possibilities. Maybe they'd have a chance to talk out their issues and finally close the door on their past. Maybe she *was* ready to come to terms with it and risk having some sort of relationship with Mason. A thrill ran through her body, bringing a smile to her face.

With his phone call, she was optimistic about the future with her mom and Katie.

Seeing Mason would be the perfect bonus.

CHAPTER SEVEN

Two DAYS LATER when Lisa arrived home, Esther, the cleaning lady her parents had had for years, was there to help her get her mother and Katie settled. Lisa had arranged to take two weeks of vacation from her job while she got her life organized. She went to see a physiotherapist to put together a physical-care plan for her mother, and hired a nursing assistant to be there for Carolyn once Lisa returned to work.

She'd never been busier, but it was a happy kind of busy, she mused as she poured coffee for her mother and herself the next day.

She glanced around at the mounds of toys, following Katie's movements as she played near the sliding glass doors leading to the patio by the pool.

She thought back to the hours in the car with her mother while they shared their pasts; all of those memories bringing them closer to each other. Lisa learned that Carolyn Lewis was a woman with a very positive attitude toward life, a trait Lisa admired.

Alice Clarke had seldom shared her past with Lisa except for her fear of taking risks and her obsession with protecting Lisa from harm. Bringing Carolyn and Katie home to Durham would have been, in Alice's opinion, a huge risk.

But Lisa was proud of what she'd done. She loved how alive and involved the whole endeavor made her feel.

As she put a mug of coffee in front of her mother, she remembered how much help Carolyn had been, especially the first night on the road when Katie cried herself to sleep.

"I'm glad we're finally home and that you and Katie are settling in. What would I have done without you these past couple of days, Mom?" she asked, astonished at how naturally the word *Mom* slipped into her question.

"You're so good with her, I'm sure you would have managed just fine. Being a pediatric nurse, you've done all this before, I suppose."

"Believe me, it's not the same," she said ruefully.

She got her mother settled in the sunroom, and sat beside her, thinking of one area which she *hadn't* managed.

"I don't understand why Katie won't sleep in her crib. The two nights we were on the road she slept with me, but I assumed that last night she'd sleep in her own bed. Perhaps I'm expecting too much after all she's been through."

"Her mother was like that. Anne Marie was nearly two before she slept through the night in her own bed.

Maybe Katie's having trouble because everything's so different, and she's almost certainly missing Anne Marie. But children adjust easily once a routine is established."

A routine. How could she not have been aware of something so fundamental to Katie's happiness?

"Of course, you're right. Katie must have been lost without her mom, and then I come along and snatch her away from everything familiar."

Lisa took a quick sip of her coffee as she watched Katie play with Nemo. "So, what do I do? Katie can't sleep with me every night. I mean, I read that children shouldn't sleep with their parents…"

Her mother reached over and rested her fingers on Lisa's arm. "Dear, don't worry about it. What Katie needs right now is the security of knowing she's loved and cared for, and you're giving her that. When she's used to her new circumstances you can consider putting her in her crib at night. Do you mind having her sleep with you?"

"No, not at all. The first couple of nights were a little difficult, but there's something so wonderful about watching a child sleep. And she likes me to read to her. I dug some of my old books out of the attic. She got me to go through one of the Seuss books twice last night before she fell asleep. My mom read to me as a child. Those are some of my fondest memories because it was just the two of us, plus my stuffed animals."

The back doorbell rang. "That must be the carpenter who's going to build the ramp," Lisa said, jumping up.

But when she answered the door, she saw Mason standing on the back step. "What are you doing here so early?" she asked, surprised.

"I came by to see if there's anything you need," he said, glancing past her. "Hello, Mrs. Lewis."

He stood there, his feet planted cop-style on the step, a challenging grin on his face. "I also wanted to know if I could drop over this evening."

"Why?" she asked, her tone sounding confrontational to her own ears.

"You'll see. Nothing sinister, just a small surprise."

"What are you up to?" she asked, gentling her tone, basking in the happy thought that Mason wanted to surprise her. Did his request mean he wanted to spend time alone with her? Were they finally going to finish their conversation from that night in the restaurant? A little late but…

"Patience is a virtue," he replied, his voice teasing.

"Would you like to come in? Mom and I are having coffee and watching Katie play."

"How can I resist an invitation like that?"

"It's simple—you can't," she said, aware of how good he looked in his black shirt and jeans.

"Is this the new take-charge Lisa? I don't think

we've met," he said, his voice intimate, making her pulse jump.

"Get used to it," she warned. As she let herself slide back into the old bantering ways, a thought popped into her mind. She'd always preferred Mason like this, more than the Mason who always had to take control.

Yet, in the beginning, when their relationship was fresh and new, she *hadn't* let him take over, she reminded herself. It was only later as they became more serious that she'd allowed him to make all the decisions for them as a couple. He had picked the restaurants and most of the movies. He didn't like the symphony, so she gave up her season tickets. He knew about cars so she bought the car he'd told her to. And somewhere along the road she'd stopped voicing her own opinions.

Had the change been that simple? Why hadn't she insisted on being part of how they decided the issues between them? After all, she had a responsible job, friends and people who sought her advice as a nurse. Had she passed control of her life to Mason without realizing it? She'd certainly seen a change in herself this past week. As difficult as it had been to have to take on so much for her new family, she liked the feeling of being in charge. She enjoyed being her own person, making decisions for her own and her family's benefit.

She'd never again be shut out of making decisions about her life.

"How about joining Mom and me for a cup of coffee?" she asked.

"I'd love one."

"Thanks for the name of the carpenter, by the way. He says he'll build the ramp and make the changes in the den so she can be more comfortable. She's sleeping on the hideaway bed in there at the moment."

Her mother wheeled into the kitchen, then stopped at the table and looked up at Mason. "I want to thank you for bringing my daughter into my life, Mason," her mother said.

"Just doing my job," he said, but Lisa could hear the pride in his voice.

She listened to the easy way Mason and her mother chatted, happy in the feeling that life had become so much more than she could ever have imagined the day she'd walked into Tank's office.

"Juice?" Katie asked in her high-pitched voice. Lisa had discovered that everything Katie said sounded like a question.

"Sure," Lisa said, going to the fridge.

"Katie, do you want to sit at the table with us?" Mason asked.

Katie searched Lisa's face for approval. As Lisa nodded, she met her niece's anxious eyes, and joy warmed every part of her.

Katie was already seeking her out and placing her

trust in her. Lisa felt a rush of contentment at the bond forming between them. Until now, Lisa had only ever read about such a thing. But experiencing it was so very different.

"Here's your juice, and I'll help you into your booster seat," she said with a confidence that hadn't been there three days ago. As Katie climbed onto the chair, Lisa was again reminded of how easy Katie was to care for…and love.

Lisa had felt so many emotions around Katie, emotions she couldn't explain to anyone, except that she was totally happy for the first time in her life.

She watched as Mason talked with Katie and she was impressed by how quickly he connected with the little girl. The longer he chatted with Katie the more she giggled.

She caught her mother's slow smile as she listened to Mason. Were there any females on planet Earth who didn't succumb to Mason's charms?

HAVING ANSWERED a dozen questions from Katie, Mason sipped his coffee. Mrs. Lewis's happiness was almost palpable while Lisa's face held a look of such contentment, it was almost impossible not to stare at her. He had to confess that he hadn't expected Lisa to be able to handle all the responsibility she'd taken on so quickly. She'd always hung back, waited to be sure about her actions. Yet here she was organizing a life for a whole new family with ease and assurance.

Lisa was responding to her changed circumstances—heart first. "I see you've got everything under control," he said, feeling left out of the happiness in the room as he listened to their delighted chatter about Katie's latest antic.

"Learning to care for Katie is a full-time job…a wonderful job." She sighed.

"Looks like you two have filled any gaps in Katie's life."

"Hope so. Keeping up with Katie on the drive back to Durham made us co-conspirators," Carolyn Lewis said, amusement evident in her voice.

"Yeah, I'm sure we didn't miss a single McDonald's on the way from Melbourne to Durham. And the ones with those play areas were like magnets," Lisa added, laughing.

Mason couldn't remember the last time he'd heard Lisa laugh with such freedom. He let his gaze travel over her face, struck with how beautiful she looked. Without a hint of makeup, dressed in blue jeans, a tight fitting tank top and sporting a dab of ketchup in her hair, she'd never been sexier.

He was in awe of the easy conversation flowing between Lisa and her mother, and witnessed the love that was so visible on their faces. A few days ago, he wouldn't have believed it possible that Lisa and her mother could become this close so quickly.

Seeing them now, it was clear they were meant

to be together, and his fears about how Lisa would manage all this were unfounded.

Lisa seemed happier and it was all because she had a family of her own. While they were dating, he'd sensed that Lisa was holding back at times, uncertain with him. As he watched her chatting with her mother and Katie, he understood that her uncertainty probably came from not knowing exactly who she was or where she'd come from.

There was something so certain in her now, as if she had a mission, a purpose beyond herself, and he was happy for her. But seeing the way she gave her undivided attention to her new family brought an unfamiliar feeling to the surface. He wished he'd been a part of this change in Lisa. If he had listened to her, been more open to her feelings and opinions, they might still be together.

Yet, as he took in the positive changes in Lisa, he could not stop the feeling that somehow he and Lisa *had* reconnected. Only this time around, the connection went much deeper.

His BlackBerry bleated with the reminder of an appointment with another new client. His business was expanding more rapidly than he'd anticipated. "I've got to go," he said, feeling genuinely sorry that he had to leave this soon.

"I'll walk you to your car," Lisa offered, getting up and following him.

IN THE YARD, shaded from the late-morning sun by a magnolia tree, Mason unlocked his car. "Things are working out for you."

"They sure are," Lisa said. She had a lot to be thankful for these days. Yet, as she met his gaze, she became acutely aware of what her life might have been like if she and Mason had married.

They would have had a child; she would've seen him off to work like this, her heart bursting with the knowledge that he loved her and their baby. "My life is so different, so changed," she said, a sudden sweep of longing making her voice thick with emotion.

As he moved closer, she could smell the scent of sun on his skin and a hint of cologne. "Are you okay?"

"Absolutely," she said, wanting to rest her hands on his chest, feel the muscles beneath the cotton shirt he wore, put her arms around his neck and kiss him.

An awkward silence rose between them. "My business is picking up," he said, a hesitant tone in his voice as he jammed his hands in the pockets of his black jeans.

"That's great. You must be pleased." She saw a look of uncertainty in his eyes. Mason uncertain? It couldn't be...

"I'd better get going," he said, pulling his hands out of his pockets and opening the car door. "If you need anything, let me know. In the meantime, remember to lock your doors and set the alarm—"

"I'm not a child," she said. It came out harsher than she'd intended, but she'd begun to feel suffocated when he went into his controlling mode. "I know you mean well," she said to soften her words.

She wanted to make her own decisions. The ones she'd made since the reading of the will had given her a great deal of pleasure—proof that she was capable of running her own life.

His glance was one of resignation. "Fine," he said, the old edge returning to his voice.

She'd hurt his feelings, but she had to make it clear that he couldn't step back into her life and try to dictate everything she did.

Annoyed with herself for handling the situation so poorly, she watched him drive down the street.

Get over it. There's no reason for you to be upset with him. He was only doing what comes naturally.

Back in the house, she busied herself with putting a load of laundry into the washer and putting the dishes into the dishwasher.

"Mason's a wonderful man. Did you date?" her mother asked.

Taken by surprise, Lisa turned to her mother. "Years ago. How did you know?"

"It shows on your face, how you behave around him. You care for him deeply—or did," her mother added.

"Yes…"

"And now?"

She shrugged, still a little uncomfortable with the whole subject of Mason. "We're friends."

"Good enough friends for him to be willing to help you get your life organized around an invalid mother and a niece who may be living with you for quite some time. That's a *very* good friend. If only Anne Marie had had a friend like that, maybe she wouldn't have gotten mixed up with the wrong crowd."

"Mom, you can't think she's guilty of anything."

"No, of course not, but appearances can be deceptive and that boyfriend of hers was a piece of work, let me tell you."

Recalling Mason's remarks about Anne Marie's dilemma, Lisa didn't want to discuss how her sister had ended up where she did. It was too nice a day, and Lisa wanted to spend every moment she could with Katie. She fervently believed that Anne Marie would be freed. And then she'd come for Katie—something Lisa had begun to dread. "Let's have lunch, and then we'll put Katie down for a nap."

A little later in Lisa's bed, she lay quietly beside Katie, studying her niece's sleeping form, from her tiny nose to the way her hands clutched her blanket. Everything about Katie thrilled her, from the squeals of delight over whatever held her attention, to the endearing look in her eyes as she climbed into Lisa's lap seeking comfort.

Listening to her even breathing and satisfied that

she was asleep, Lisa eased from the bed only to hear Katie cry out as she reached her arms up to Lisa.

"I want Mommy," she cried, her body trembling. "I want Mommy."

Lisa gathered her in her arms, checking her forehead for any sign of fever. "You'll see Mommy soon," she whispered into her hair.

"Where's Mommy?" Katie asked as she began sucking her thumb while she hiccuped and snuggled closer to Lisa. "Bad dream." She sniffled and rubbed her face into Lisa's shoulder.

She couldn't bear to hear Katie cry for her mother, especially when there were no promises she could make. And what if Katie continued to cry? She hugged her tightly, smoothing the blond curls from her face.

Hoping she'd gone back to sleep, she peeked at Katie's face and was disappointed to see that the little girl's eyes were wide-open, her expression watchful.

"I won't leave you," she said, placing the blankets over the child and climbing in beside her again. Katie wriggled closer, warming Lisa where they touched—a warmth that relieved Lisa's apprehensions. She closed her eyes, breathing in the sweet scent of the child's skin, listening to Katie as she sucked her thumb. As she cradled Katie, she imagined how she'd feel if Katie were her daughter…

Feeling a sense of loss she'd never experienced

before, Lisa clung to the idea that she had a family who needed her. And the little person she held so close to her would require all the love and care she could offer while they waited for Anne Marie's release.

She refused to let her worries about whether she could look after Katie ruin this joy.

EARLY THAT EVENING, Lisa put the phone down, her hands shaking as she tried to control her excitement. The nursing supervisor had called to tell her that the hospital wanted her to take over as head nurse of Pediatrics.

"Mom, guess what?"

"What?" her mother asked, wheeling her way out of the den toward the kitchen.

"I just got offered the position of head nurse on Pediatrics. I never imagined I'd get the job. It took them so long to decide, and I was so nervous in the interview. It must have gone better than I thought, and I suppose they had a lot of applicants and red tape to go through."

"Congratulations! I'm so happy for you."

"Thanks, Mom." But now that the job was hers, she had misgivings. She'd never put herself out there like this before. There would be a lot of responsibility and scrutiny. Did she want it?

"You and Mason will have a lot to celebrate when he gets here. What time did he say?"

Lisa checked her watch, assessing her wrinkled pink shirt and blue jeans. "Oh! No! In five minutes, and I'm not ready. Not a bit of makeup. How bad do I look?"

"You look lovely. Absolutely radiant. I love you, my darling daughter," her mother said, maneuvering her chair over to the counter where Lisa stood.

"I love you, too, Mom." Still not accustomed to having a mother who expressed her emotions so easily, she leaned down and kissed her mother's cheek. "A new mom, a new niece and now the possibility of a new job. Life doesn't get much better than this."

"What would make it perfect would be Mason coming over here for some serious personal talk about the two of you," her mother said.

"No, I doubt that very much. Mason has a full life, and he's simply helping out a friend."

"A mother can still dream," she said, a smug look on her face.

"Well, in the meantime, you relax and enjoy yourself. When Mason comes, we'll be out by the pool, and I'll have the baby monitor with me in case Katie wakes up."

"I'll be in the den if you need me."

The front doorbell chimed, and Lisa rushed to answer it. Through the side glass panels, she could see Mason standing there looking handsome in a sky-blue shirt and navy pants with a bottle of champagne resting in the crook of his arm.

Could her mother be right? *Did* Mason want to try again? And if so, could they start over?

She opened the door. Mason remained motionless for a moment, a smile lifting the corners of his mouth.

"You're the picture of happiness," he murmured as he brought his arms around her.

He felt good. He smelled good. But she wasn't sure how to respond. Was the hug merely a friendly gesture? Or something more? Before she could move, he stepped back and held out the champagne.

"This is your night. We're going to celebrate."

"You have news, too?"

For a moment he looked startled. "No. I wanted to surprise you with a bottle of bubbly to toast the new take-charge Lisa."

Now it was her turn to be startled. She *had* changed but she didn't think he'd noticed. "Oh, thank you. I do feel like I'm headed in a different direction in my life. I have something exciting to tell you."

"You do?" he asked, following her to the kitchen. He took the ice bucket from the cupboard over the fridge, filled it with ice and put the bottle in. He did it all as naturally as if this were his kitchen…their kitchen.

"You're not going to believe this. Let's go out by the pool. I'll get the glasses."

"My kind of woman," he kidded.

They settled into the wrought-iron chairs with a small table separating them. The night air was warm with the scent of basil growing in the herb garden Alice had carefully maintained for years.

Lisa waited while Mason poured two glasses, the bubbles as bright as her happiness. "A couple of months ago, I applied for a promotion as head nurse of Pediatrics. I just found out I got it!"

"Congratulations!" He raised his glass. "To Lisa, the boss on Pediatrics."

"Though I haven't said I'll accept the position yet. I thought I wanted it but now I'm not sure it's a good idea."

He lowered his glass. "Why not?"

"I've really enjoyed nursing children, but—"

"But what?" he asked, his features softened by the reflected light of the pool.

"I still hear my mother's voice in my head, and for better or worse, I'm listening."

"And that voice tells you to be cautious and circumspect, especially around children."

"That's about it," she said, feeling closer to Mason than she had in so long. She wanted to reach out to him, have him touch her skin. Instead, she clutched the stem of her champagne flute for the little support it offered.

When he didn't say anything, she nervously gulped

her champagne, feeling the effects all the way to her toes.

"Lisa, you're one of the smartest, most determined people I've ever known. If you decide to take on this new position, you'll make an excellent head nurse."

"And will that finally silence my mother's voice?"

He grinned. "Definitely."

But would it erase the memory, the fear, of that night with Linda Jean Bemrose? "I wish I was as sure as you are."

"Give yourself time. Take a chance. You've already taken a major one in your personal life, and look what it's done for you." His gaze moved over her face, to her lips and back to her eyes. "What are you thinking about?" he asked.

He edged toward her, the heat of his body mingling with hers. He was so close, his lips so near. Would he kiss her? The soothing tone, the shimmering light from the pool and the heady effects of the champagne joined forces. "So much has happened... between us."

"Do you wish for more?" he asked.

He wanted her, his eyes said so. Yet she couldn't offer him more when her life was so unsettled. She leaned away from him. "I'm not sure," she replied.

He averted his gaze. His champagne flute clinked as it touched down on the table.

She tried to explain. "I'll admit there have been

times, but you wanted the whole picture—children, the house, the supportive wife. However, my picture and yours weren't the same. And it wasn't just the issue of children. There were moments when it seemed like you'd taken over my life. I'm sure you meant well, but I felt trapped."

He poured more champagne for both of them. "Go on."

Taking a giant sip, she leaned across the table. "You expect things to happen your way. I grew up in a house where what my parents wanted usually came ahead of what I wanted, and I didn't argue very often. So you see, I began to resent your advice, no matter how well-intentioned."

She hiccuped. *No! She couldn't be drunk!* Her cheeks flamed in embarrassment.

His expression solemn, he reached across the table and took her hand. "Lisa, if I could change only one thing in my life, it would be that night we broke up. By the time I realized what a mistake I'd made, it was too late. Yet being with you again recently has made me realize what I lost. You and I had a great thing, but I was so busy doing things my way, I ignored what you needed."

"We both made mistakes," she conceded.

"Lisa." He shifted in his chair. "I had this plan for tonight. I wanted it to be a celebration of your success with your new family. And to apologize for doubting you."

"What's that got to do with you and me, in the personal sense, I mean?" she asked, hopeful that they were going to talk about that night.

He grimaced. "I had a phone call from Sara before I left. I'm guessing you've heard the rumors about her music career."

She nodded, a sick feeling swimming in her stomach.

"It looks like she'll be moving to L.A. Nothing's signed yet, so there's always a chance she won't go. I'm not sure where that leaves me with regard to Peter," he said, his voice trailing off.

Was he seriously considering moving to L.A.? "What will you do?" she asked, easing her hand from his.

"I'm not sure. I mean, I may have to rethink my life…change my plans, maybe. At this point, who knows?"

She wanted to be there for him, to offer comfort. Having Katie in her life, she empathized with Mason. "Can I help?"

"I wish you could. But I don't know if I can live without Peter. L.A. is so far away. My visits with him would be quite limited if I don't move. And then there's us. I don't want to leave you just when we're getting closer to each other again. I'm torn."

She tried to say she felt the same way but the words wouldn't leave her lips. They'd gotten closer, but not enough for her to risk another rejection. She'd wanted to explain why she'd reacted the way she had the night they'd broken up, to tell him how humiliated she'd been when he'd walked out. To say how cautious she had become after all her plans and dreams had been swept away so easily, so quickly. But given his news and the upheaval in her own life, she held back. She tucked her hands into her lap as tears blurred her vision.

"Please don't cry," he said, his voice thick.

If only she hadn't drunk the champagne—her head was fuzzy. "You'd better leave. I don't want Mom to see that I'm upset. She'll worry," she said, her chest hurting from the pressure of wanting to cry... in private.

He lifted a hand to touch her hair.

She moved away from him.

In the dim light of the pool, his face held an intense look of sadness Lisa hadn't seen before. "I'll go out the back way so as not to upset your mom."

For a few minutes there was only the sound of the pool pump humming.

HE WAITED FOR HER to say what he needed to hear—that she understood what he was going through. But he had no right to expect her to understand when he was so confused himself. He couldn't face moving out west, leaving Lisa just when they were getting somewhere. He couldn't grasp the idea of moving thousands of miles away to a strange city, starting over, in the hope of staying in daily contact with his son.

On the other hand, he couldn't see his life without Peter.

There had to be a better way. He had to convince Sara that Peter was better off here with him and his family.

He'd tried to talk to her about that, but she was totally preoccupied with her newfound success.

His whole life was one big mix-up, but that wasn't Lisa's problem. He'd find a solution, and if it meant leaving Durham for L.A., well, he'd have to make the best of it. Leaving Peter was not an option.

Until then, he had no business offering her anything but his friendship.

"I'm going now."

She didn't follow him to the door.

CHAPTER EIGHT

FIGHTING TO KEEP her thoughts away from what Mason had said last night, Lisa sang along with her mother and Katie as they drove back from the appointment at the rehab center. Anything to quell the anxiety percolating in her stomach. "So, you had a good appointment with Dr. Morgan, Mom?"

"I did. He's marvelous. I feel so much better, and the therapy pool was wonderful," Carolyn said, a look of appreciation in her eyes.

"Our pool's ready to go, and once the carpenter's finished in the house, you'll be able to live a pretty normal life," Lisa said, pulling into the driveway.

"I don't know how to thank you."

"There's no need, Mom. Having you here is thanks enough." Lisa picked Katie up and hugged her close, thankful that Katie was part of her life. How her feelings had changed since that day in the jail!

Supporting Katie on one hip, she slipped the key into the lock in the back door.

The sound of a car in the driveway caught her attention.

"Thought I'd drop by and see how you ladies are

doing," Mason called out, striding toward them as if nothing had happened last night.

His hair was damp and clinging to his neck, and his open shirt exposed the gold chain he always wore as he expertly helped Carolyn into her wheelchair and pushed her ahead of him toward the door.

"We didn't expect to see you so soon," Lisa said, a questioning tone in her voice as he wheeled Carolyn up the ramp.

He looked startled for a moment as he touched Lisa's shoulder. "I couldn't stay away."

She saw the warmth in his eyes. The air between them vibrated with emotion, and she felt like the only woman on earth.

"Katie and I were about to play with the Barbie dolls we bought today," she said to hide her reaction.

"You're going to spoil her," Carolyn warned.

Mason stepped back, holding the door for Lisa and her mother. "You sound more energetic today, Mrs. Lewis," he said.

"Call me Carolyn, please. Yes, I was pretty tired when you were here last night. I fell asleep before you left. Did you kids have a nice evening?" she asked as she wheeled into the sunroom.

"Yes, we did," Mason responded as he reached to take Katie from Lisa's arms.

She couldn't help noticing how easily he fit into her family. And she couldn't blame Katie and her mother for being happy to see him, but their happiness wouldn't last if he decided to move to L.A.

Yet having him standing there beside her smoothed away some of the tension that had knotted her neck all morning.

She was brought back to the present when Katie began to squirm in Mason's arms. "Down!" she called out, a mischievous grin on her face.

"What do you want, kid?" he asked with a fake growl, lowering her to the carpet.

Within minutes he was on the floor with her, helping her undo the packaging of her new Barbie dolls. "Wow, someone's been shopping," he said, glancing up at Lisa.

"Couldn't resist."

"Who can?" They laughed together.

She'd miss Mason if he decided to go. She'd miss his comfortable manner with children, the many times they'd laughed about the silliest things, the excitement of being near him.

But most of all, even after last night, their stiffness around each other seemed to have evaporated. The old back-and-forth that had existed between them, the innate trust they shared, had resurfaced.

Only now it was too late. She simply couldn't see how Mason would be able to stay in Durham with his son on the West Coast.

Which meant that he'd carefully choose a time to

talk to her about his decision—before he walked out of her life.

They chatted for a while as Mason sat on the floor of the sunroom, playing with Katie. With a squeal of enthusiasm, she plunked one of her Barbie dolls on Mason's head.

"Hey, kiddo, you could ruin my good looks."

"No!" Katie gave him another thump with her Barbie, this time on his shoulder.

"Have you heard from Anne Marie's lawyer?" he asked.

"Not since our meeting, and I'm a little concerned. I was hoping he'd call with an update."

"These things take time."

"I'll call him if I don't hear anything in the next couple of days."

"So, what's next for Ms. Katie?" Mason asked as he got up off the floor and sat down next to Lisa.

"A bath. We stopped at the playground on the way home from Mom's physio. I've got to put Katie in the tub, but you chat with Mom for a bit. I'll be back in a few minutes."

"Go with Aunt Lisa," her mother said to Katie.

"No bath. I want Mommy. I want Mommy!"

Not again. "Katie, your mommy's busy right now, but I'm sure she'll call us as soon as she can," Lisa said, her stomach tensing.

"Tell you what, Katie. How about we play with the dolphin in the tub?" Mason suggested.

"No bath." She planted her little fists on her hips, suspicion furrowing her brows.

Mason winked at Lisa over Katie's head. "No bath, just some fun in the water. You want to be able to swim in the big pool, don't you?" he asked, lifting Katie into his arms.

"Yeah, I love the pool," Katie said, a businesslike look on her tiny face. "I swim."

"That's great. We'll start with a splash session in the tub," Mason said, making his way down the hall to the foot of the stairs. "Coming, Lisa?"

"So Peter's father is an expert on bathing children," she murmured.

"If you'd been willing to babysit my nieces and nephews with me, you'd have seen up close and personal just what an expert I am on kid-related activities."

Having Katie now, she wished she had gone to babysit with him, or at least tried to. Having him back in her life reminded her of the jokes they'd shared, the barbecues for two they'd held in his backyard, the long conversations. But most of all, she could still feel his arms around her as they finished cleaning up in the kitchen, the way he kissed her neck as his hands explored her body.

With Katie peering over his shoulder at Lisa, they went upstairs.

"Hold her while I run the tub and get the show under way. Do you have baby shampoo?" he asked as they entered the oversize bathroom with the giant Jacuzzi tub.

"Right there." She pointed to where all the personal-care products were lined up at the back of the tub.

"I should have known. Are these alphabetized?"

"And what if they are?" she said, raising her eyebrows. In the past, he'd never missed an opportunity to make fun of her need for order, everything from making lists to organizing cupboards.

Sitting on the bench beside the tub, she eased Katie out of her clothes while she watched Mason get the bath ready.

Lisa wasn't sure who was clinging to whom as she tried to adjust Katie's tiny body against hers before she knelt in front of the tub.

"Here, let me help you," he said, holding out his arms.

His hands touched hers as he took Katie from her and her body warmed in response to the wet heat of his skin. In the intimacy of her bathroom, she couldn't look at him, couldn't let him see how much something as casual as his touch affected her.

"Okay, Katie. Let's show Dolphin how it's done," he said, lowering her into the water and picking up a little rubber dolphin to play with.

For a moment she howled in protest, and Lisa was sure they were in for another round of Katie calling for her mother.

"Can you swim like the dolphin?" he asked, racing the toy through the water to delighted squeals from Katie.

Leaning over the tub in such close proximity to Mason, all she could think about was how close his arms were to hers as he gently splashed Katie. His tenderness and the way he related to Katie made Lisa's breath catch in her throat.

The man being so gentle with Katie was in such contrast to the one who had faced danger as a police officer, and who loved the speed of a motorcycle.

A flood of need, visceral and undeniable, swept through her. She had to get up, get out, away from him, do anything but succumb. "Time to get out, sweetie."

"No!" Katie yelled, slapping the water with both hands.

"Please," Lisa said, placing her hands around Katie's slippery body. Just as Lisa got a good grip on her, Katie twisted free and slipped facedown in the water.

"Oh, no," Lisa moaned, trying to get a firm handle on the struggling child, who popped up out of the water, screaming.

"Pick her up," Mason yelled over the din. "Like this," he said, holding his hands around Lisa's as he helped lift the crying child from the tub.

Attempting to quiet her, she patted Katie's back and snuggled her.

"Here, try putting the towel around her so you don't get soaked through." Mason placed the towel around Katie's shoulders, his fingers brushing Lisa's breasts.

Red heat crawled over her face, but he didn't seem to notice as he returned his attention to the tub, removing the toys and pulling the plug.

It was a simple task and he did it with such ease, his broad shoulders within her reach. The intimate way he glanced back at her as he wrung out the facecloth and put it on the edge of the tub added to the feeling of warmth and coziness.

She and Mason had spent so many ordinary days together, doing what any couple would do, but none of those moments had felt quite like this.

She loved the way Mason cared for her new family. And despite his earlier grumpiness over what she'd taken on, in her heart she realized that Mason would always support her.

For the past five years, she'd wondered if they'd ever be part of each other's life again.

They were for now, but if he moved to L.A. they'd face another separation—this time a permanent one.

In the meantime, they were friends, a much safer connection, and one she could handle.

LISA HOLDING A CHILD in her arms... How many times had he imagined this scene as part of their marriage? He was filled with a sense of loss so powerful it took his breath away. He'd wanted to have children with this woman, and she'd been unable, for reasons he'd never entirely understood, to agree.

"Now, we're ready for clean clothes," Lisa said, nuzzling Katie's cheek. As he followed them to Katie's bedroom, he couldn't help noticing how quickly Lisa had taken to motherhood. As she dressed Katie in purple shorts and matching top, his mind drifted back to the evening they broke up.

He'd been shocked at first by her response. Shock had turned to anger, at himself and at the world in general. In retrospect, he'd just assumed she was aware he wanted children, but more importantly, that she would naturally want them, as well. His vision of their life together had been smashed by her refusal to even discuss the issue of children.

He'd held on to his anger for five long years. But when Lisa picked Katie up and turned to him, he forgot all about it. Despite everything that had happened between them, he still wanted to be with her....

But he'd never again make the mistake of assuming that she wanted what he wanted.

As they stood shoulder to shoulder, his arms ached to hold her, to feel her warmth, to kiss her. He leaned toward her, hoping she'd glance up at him. When she did, her eyes met his, her lips parted. If he kissed her now, it would be more than a kiss between friends.

And with his uncertain future, he had no right to get involved with her. He'd walked out on her before and hurt her. He wouldn't do it again.

They'd lost so much that night he'd insisted children be part of their marriage plans. She had refused and he'd walked out. But what choice did he have? He couldn't face a life without children.

He smiled ruefully. That was why he'd have to make some major changes now or he'd face exactly that. A life without his son.

"What's that smile about?" she asked.

Trying to ease the confusion roaring through him, he said, "I believe you're better at parenting than you thought."

She lifted Katie higher up in her arms. "Maybe, but it's all so new." She kissed Katie's curls and Mason's heart leaped in his chest at the sight and at the feelings of loss charging through him.

"You'll be fine," he said, searching for an excuse to leave, to get the hell out before he said something she wasn't ready to hear.

"Thanks for everything," Lisa said, letting Katie down.

They stood so close he noticed the faint line of freckles on her nose. "Anytime."

Regardless of what might have been, or what he felt about her behavior that night, the one fact he had to accept was that he'd never gotten over her.

The shameful truth was that he'd married Sara because she was pregnant and not out of love.

UNABLE TO CALM her racing pulse at the stark intensity she'd seen in his eyes, Lisa stood waiting for Mason to move away. She'd never had a connection to him like this, a connection she couldn't identify. Was it the moment with Katie? Their experience of caring for a little girl who needed them?

Her body warmed at a sense of being whole, of feeling a part of something special. Something she shared with Mason. As they stood near to each other, Lisa felt the old yearning to talk about what had happened between them.

But Mason wasn't the kind of man who spent time on self-examination, and in her experience he'd never once reconsidered a decision.

His fingers touched her chin. "I should get back to the office," he murmured, his lips inches from hers. "I enjoyed every minute."

"I did, too," she said, waiting for his mouth to take hers.

Instead, he scooped Katie into his arms, kissed her cheeks and tousled her hair. "See you soon, Katie," he said, passing her to Lisa. Before she could respond, he was out of the room and heading down the stairs.

She lifted Katie up for a piggyback ride, then followed Mason down to the sunroom. She heard him say goodbye to her mother.

"Wait for us," she called, jostling Katie as she tried to catch up with him.

His tall frame was silhouetted by the sunlight glinting off the surface of the pool, and when she caught up with him, she saw that the teasing look was back in his eyes. Teasing looks she could deal with, but just to be sure, she moved to a safe subject.

"How's business?" she asked, sliding Katie to the floor.

"Going well. In fact, I'm busy enough that I might not be able to check on your progress for a few days."

Disappointment lurked in the corner of her mind. "You make it sound like I'm an experiment."

"You could say that," he said, giving her a once-over she felt right down to her toes.

"Should I be happy about my new role? As an experiment, I mean." She smiled, trying to keep the conversation light and impersonal, while she recognized how much she'd miss him.

He's not going to Siberia... But he may be going to L.A. "Tell you what," she added. "When you've got time, why don't we set a playdate for Peter and Katie? I'd love to meet Peter and get to know him."

His eyebrows jumped. "A date for the kids."

Did he think she was using Katie as a way to see him? "It's only a suggestion...if you'd like to."

With a hint of a smile, he said, "That would be wonderful. The kids will have a great time. And, Lisa, I'm glad to see this change in you…around children, I mean. I'll call you later this evening. Peter would love to play in the pool. Why don't you walk out to the car with me and we can discuss it?"

Surprise filtered through her. Was he going to talk about how she'd changed and what that meant to him? Or was he going to tell her what he'd decided to do about L.A.? Did she want to know right now—and possibly ruin the day?

She glanced back toward the sunroom where her mother and Katie were working on a puzzle, her mother's gray hair a sharp contrast to Katie's lighter curls. It was a scene she'd never expected to see in her lifetime, and she'd had no idea how much she'd love it.

She couldn't influence Sara and Mason's decision. Deep down she knew Mason couldn't stay in Durham without Peter. So that settled it—if Sara did indeed go to California, as seemed likely. Today wasn't a day for bad news. Tomorrow or next week would be soon enough.

"Can we talk later? I really need to get Katie's snack, and Mom needs to lie down for a rest."

"Whatever you say." Holding the back door

open, he gazed down at her. "But we do need to talk soon."

The roar of his sports car as he pulled out of the driveway punctuated her sense of foreboding.

CHAPTER NINE

SHE HADN'T SEEN MASON for three days and she'd missed him. How easily her life had begun to revolve around him, the old pattern reasserting itself. She had to admit she wanted to be with him, but there was still so much between them—both old and new problems. Still, when Mason had called to set up the playdate, she'd eagerly accepted. She'd shopped for food, a bathing suit and made sure Katie was properly outfitted. And now that the day was here, Lisa was excited.

She'd never met Peter, but she was certain that he and Katie would have fun together.

Lisa woke up, listening for any sound of Katie. Lisa's mornings were so different now with two people in the house who needed and loved her. Feeling contented and relaxed for the first time since her mother's death, she got up and tiptoed to Katie's room.

"Oh, you're awake," she said, seeing Katie peeking through the railing of the crib.

"I want up," Katie said, holding her arms out to Lisa, who eagerly gathered her close. This was the best part of Lisa's day—standing here holding Katie, feeling the little arms tighten around her neck as she snuggled, still not fully awake.

Last night after Lisa cuddled with Katie in her bed, she'd been able to put Katie in her crib, and the child had slept there all night.

"Are you hungry? What about French toast?"

Katie nodded enthusiastically.

After breakfast, Lisa prepared the lunch that she'd serve when Mason and Peter arrived. She checked on Katie, who was playing with her stuffed animals, organizing them on the kitchen table and chattering away to them. It was clear from the conversation— which included their responses—that Katie had a lively imagination.

Lisa's mother was sitting on the lounge near the pool, reading and resting. It filled Lisa with pleasure and a sense of purpose to know she'd made such a difference in Carolyn's life.

A sharp knock at the back door made her smile in anticipation. "Come in," she called, wiping her hands on a towel before answering.

When Katie saw Mason she ran toward him, her little hands waving in the air, only to stop short when she saw Peter in his arms.

"How's my girl?" Mason said. For a second, Lisa thought he meant *her*. But when he knelt down and drew Katie and Peter into a hug, Lisa felt her cheeks flush.

Katie promptly popped her thumb into her mouth as she stared uneasily at Peter, who stared back before giving a smile of glee. The little boy had his father's dark hair and quick smile, and Lisa could see the love on Mason's face.

As she stood watching them, she felt drawn into the circle of love that emanated from Mason, his arms full of children. When had her feelings changed? Just a few weeks ago she would have shied away from a scene like this.

"You look happy," she said.

"So do you. This whole fill-in mother thing has changed you…" He grinned. "See what you've been missing?"

"Yeah, I do," she replied. Swallowing a sudden lump that had risen in her throat, she glanced away.

"Anything wrong?" he asked, genuine concern in his voice.

"No." Struggling to remain calm and not blurt out her regret that she hadn't had the courage to fight for the man she'd loved or confront her fears before, she eased away.

"What's first today?" she asked, forcing herself to concentrate on the present.

"If you can take the kids, I'll bring in my stuff from the car. I got Katie a set of water wings just like Peter's, and I have a hamper of food my mother insisted on sending along."

"That was so sweet of her, but I've got all kinds of food."

"You know my mother—the more food, the better," he said, carrying both children to the kitchen and putting them in chairs before turning back to her.

He looked her over and she recognized the glint of awareness in his eyes. "How's it going?" he asked in a near whisper as he came toward her.

"It's great. Mom played with Katie last evening while I got dinner. Her treatments are going really well. Katie is so much fun, and I can't wait to get to know Peter better. I'm really enjoying myself." She heard herself babbling, and wondered if he realized how unbelievably happy she was to see him.

"It would seem my job here is done," he said with a laugh, but the underlying resignation in his tone forced her eyes to his.

"Do you think you aren't needed here anymore?" she asked, and saw by the unguarded expression on his face that she'd hit a nerve.

"Mason, there never was a point in our relationship when I didn't need you," she said, sucking in her breath in surprise at her own admission.

"I'm glad to hear you say that," he responded.

"Look, I know you're waiting to see if Sara is going to L.A., and I've probably picked the worst time to say this…"

"Go on," he said, his voice low and controlled.

"Over the past few weeks, I've come to realize that you weren't entirely to blame for what happened that night. I could have explained better."

"And I shouldn't have walked out." He gave a long sigh and ran his fingers through his hair. "So where does that leave us?"

"I wish we could have a second chance, but until the thing with L.A. gets resolved...I don't know."

"Would you consider moving to L.A.?"

Lisa wanted to say yes, but then she thought about her mother, just starting to thrive, and Katie, though she had no idea how long Katie would be with her. "No, I couldn't, not now. That's probably not what you want to hear, but it's the truth."

He reached for her, pulled her into his arms and kissed her. "I'll take the truth anytime."

As HE HELD HER, he thought over what she'd said about the night of their breakup and his mind spun at the possibility that they might be able to talk about that evening. "We have so much we need to work out," he remarked.

She pushed away and looked up into his face. "Where do we start?" she asked tentatively.

Don't blow this. Discussing it here, with her mother and Katie to interrupt, wasn't such a good idea. "Let's see, we could go to dinner and talk, if you'd like."

"We could… Do you think you'd be able to take an evening off?" she asked.

Go slowly. "Let me check my schedule and get back to you."

Her answering smile had him wanting to shout his pleasure. Seeking calm, he glanced over at Peter and Katie, who were playing with her collection of stuffed animals. Katie, in her bright pink bathing suit, was directing Peter, who was doing his best to arrange the animals to suit Katie.

"Katie's in charge," he said, moving the conversation to a safe topic. "Why don't I get the children ready for the pool? I see your mom's enjoying the fresh air." He nodded toward the pool where Carolyn sat in a lounge chair.

"She's enjoying everything. She's easy to please. I love doing things for her because she's so upbeat, so willing to try. Only this morning, she was telling me she hopes her rehab plan will include pool exercises because she wants to get back into swimming. Can you believe it?" she asked with enthusiasm.

He saw the light in her eyes, the hopeful tone in her voice, and realized what a powerful force Carolyn Lewis had become in Lisa's life. Lisa was changing before his eyes, from someone who saw only the problem, to someone who delighted in the solution. "You've come a long way," he said before he could stop himself.

"What do you mean?" she asked with a tiny frown.

"I mean the old Lisa would never have been willing to take on a new family, learn to cope with a child and find so much happiness in all of it."

She bit her lip and tucked a strand of hair behind her ear, a nervous reaction he was intimately familiar with.

She was about to say something when the children interrupted with their demand to go to the pool.

"Okay, you two, this is it," he said, looking at Lisa before he took their outstretched hands and led them onto the deck, grabbing the bag of pool gear on his way out through the sliding glass doors.

The sun beat down as he shrugged out of his golf shirt and shorts, and adjusted the waist of his swim trunks. Putting water wings on each of the children while they giggled and laughed, he brought them to the shallow end of the pool.

"How good of you to take time out of your busy schedule to entertain my granddaughter," Carolyn Lewis said from her lounge chair.

"No problem. This is my day with Peter, and I want to make the most of it. Swimming's the perfect activity for this weather." He smiled at her and then at the bright blue sky, immediately aware of how happy he was feeling.

He'd just gotten both children into their water wings and onto the steps at the shallow end when

Lisa appeared, wearing a white bathing suit that fit every curve of her body perfectly. He sucked in a breath at the sight of her.

"Want to join us?" he asked over the familiar rush of heat. Lisa had to be the single most gorgeous woman he'd ever seen in a bathing suit, and what made her even sexier was that she seemed completely unconscious of her impact.

"I can't wait," she said, clutching the rail as she moved down into the water. They crouched together at the bottom of the steps, each holding a child splashing in the water. And all the while, Mason was urgently aware of Lisa's body touching his.

"Do you like being with Katie?" he asked, paying close attention to where his hands were.

Lisa gave him a quick glance. "She's the sweetest child. Aren't you, Katie?" she asked, taking the little girl into her arms as naturally as any mother would.

Watching her, Mason tried not to think about how different their lives might have been if Lisa had found her mother and sister before he'd asked her to marry him.

"The best day of my life was the day Peter was born," he said as he sank into the water with his son in his arms. "Peter taught me that loving someone unselfishly is the very best kind of happiness."

Had he really said that? He was accustomed to keeping his personal feelings about love and life to himself, but being here with Lisa made him want to share his deepest thoughts.

But she didn't respond to his openness, leaving him feeling exposed, vulnerable...uncomfortable.

When he was about to give up waiting for her response, she said, "I understand what you're saying about happiness. My life has changed in ways I would never have believed a few weeks ago. I have this overwhelming urge to make sure Katie has every possible advantage until she's back with her mother. And I hope to convince Anne Marie to move here to Durham."

"That way, you'll have Katie in your life every day, is that it?" he asked, seeing the sincerity in her eyes as she spoke of her plans for the little girl who, in Mason's estimation, had created a miracle.

"When Anne Marie asked me to take Katie, I was terrified I'd make a mistake, or I'd do something wrong that would hurt Katie. I wanted everything to be perfect."

"You haven't heard?"

"Heard what?"

"Perfection and children don't go together."

"Stop teasing," she said, tilting an eyebrow at him. "But you're right about the perfection thing. Nothing's ever quite the way you expect it to be."

"Isn't that what's so great about it?" he asked, appreciating how easily they had slipped back into sharing their thoughts, that feeling of closeness.

She cocked her head to one side as she smiled at him. "Don't I know it! It's the unexpected stuff that makes it all so special."

Like a kick in the chest, he was forced to admit how much he'd missed the intimacy he'd had with Lisa.

Until the issue of children had wiped it all away.

Had they both avoided the subject out of their separate fears? But he'd never feared having children. So why hadn't he asked her long before any discussion of marriage?

As the children shrieked and played, he shoved the past away and decided to enjoy this moment. Ducking down in the water, he blew bubbles at Katie, who promptly splashed him.

"You're a monkey," he said, pulling her into his arms and spinning her around to even more shrieks of laughter.

"Am not!" she said, accompanied by a shrill scream.

He sat her on the edge of the pool then grabbed Peter, whirling him around and producing more screams and laughter.

"Wow! That's enough. My ears are hurting." He put Peter back on the pool step, his pleas for more ringing in his ears.

"Why don't you have a swim? I'll watch the children for a few minutes," she offered.

"Hey, you first. It's your pool."

"I'm not much of a swimmer."

"You'll have to learn if you're going to keep up with Katie." He nodded toward the little girl, sitting on a step, her hands smacking the water, her squeals of laughter melding with Peter's.

"It's really getting warm," she said, lifting her blond hair up off her neck. She leaned her head back, her eyes closed as she fanned her hair over her hands.

Driven by compulsion beyond his control, Mason's eyes followed the movement of her fingers, remembering how it felt to run his hands through her hair.

Her gaze caught his, drawing him like a magnet.

"I'm going to do a few lengths. I'll get out and join you in a few minutes," he said, lowering his overheated body into the water and doing the crawl stroke all the way to the other end of the pool. When he surfaced, he glanced back to see her looking at him.

He wanted to be alone with Lisa. He'd make that dinner reservation the minute he got back to the office.

CHAPTER TEN

LISA WATCHED HIM, his powerful arms slashing through the water, his dark hair shining in the midday light. She remembered how those arms had once held her.

"I hungry," Katie said, pulling at Lisa's hand.

"You are?" Lisa took her hand. "Are you and Peter ready to come in for lunch?"

They both nodded. "Mom, I'm going to take the kids in and give them lunch. Will you be okay out here?"

"I'm great, and the sun on my legs is heaven. If I change my mind, I'm sure Mason will help me. You go ahead."

Once inside, Katie insisted on macaroni and cheese. Lisa made some for her and Peter and put juice boxes out for each of them. She'd been surprised to discover that Katie's favorite meal was so simple. But she'd been surprised at a lot of things about Katie, most of all the way Katie never missed a chance to climb into her lap or sit beside her while she and Carolyn chatted.

Lisa had never expected to feel as close to Katie

as she did. Of course, her decision to take Katie had been so sudden, she hadn't had time to think about it.

The sliding doors opened and Mason came toward her, smelling of sweat and pool, his wet hair plastered to his head. "What's for lunch?"

"I put together sandwiches for us and I can't wait to dig into the pie your mother sent, but you're too late for the specialty of the day."

"Look, Daddy," Peter said, pointing to his plate.

"Ah, the way to a man's heart probably started with the invention of macaroni and cheese," he said, opening the fridge and taking out a beer. The action was so familiar, so easy, that Lisa stopped, shaken by a swift flood of yearning.

"What is it?" Mason asked.

All the regret over what might have been—and the hope of what still could be—rendered her speechless. She wouldn't look at him, feeling the way she did right now. How could something so simple make her want to cry? It was over. They had their friendship— a good one. But no matter what label she put on it, she'd still be devastated if he moved to L.A.

What was wrong with her? She drew in a deep breath and managed to utter the words, "Just thinking I should bring Mom in for lunch." She darted past the kids out to the deck.

Needing to escape the confined space of the kitchen and Mason's questioning glance, she strode around the pool toward her mother, who was still sitting in the sun. "Do you want something to eat now, Mom?"

"That would be wonderful," her mother said, turning to look at Lisa. "Honey, what's wrong?"

"Nothing," Lisa said, bringing the wheelchair closer to the lounger so she could transfer her mother.

"'Nothing' wouldn't make your eyes red."

"Chlorine would, though," Lisa said, determined not to admit how upset she was. Her mother had enough on her mind.

"Weesa!" Katie squealed gleefully.

Distracted, Lisa glanced behind her. Katie was running dangerously near the edge of the pool. "Katie! Stop!"

Fear knotting her stomach, Lisa raced toward her.

"Weesa!" Katie screamed as she tripped and fell face-first into the water.

"Mason!" Lisa yelled as she jumped in after her. Lisa sank below the surface for a moment, but by the time she cleared the water from her eyes, she could see Katie a few feet from her, flailing in the water and screaming. She swam as fast as she could, grabbing Katie by the straps of her tiny swimsuit.

Doing her best to tread water, tears flooding her eyes and her heart pounding in her chest, Lisa struggled to reach the edge of the pool with Katie writhing frantically in her arms.

Suddenly Mason was beside her, taking Katie from her trembling arms. Without a word, he held Katie while his powerful kicks propelled him to the shallow end where he climbed out of the pool.

"She's okay, Lisa," he said, calmly and with complete certainty. She clung to his words, drawing on his strength.

He wrapped Katie in a towel while he murmured soothing words to her. Relief ran through Lisa as she forced her arms and legs to move toward the end of the pool.

When she got there, Katie refused her outstretched arms and instead snuggled into Mason's shoulder, her little body shuddering as she clung to him.

Lisa fought back tears of remorse. Because of her, Katie had nearly drowned. "If only I hadn't left the sliding glass doors open," she said, her voice shaking. "How stupid could I be?"

"*Stupid* is a bad word," Katie said over her sobs.

"Where did you learn that?" Mason said, looking into Katie's face and chucking her under the chin, his behavior reassuring.

"Cindy says it's bad."

"That's the lady who was looking after Katie when I picked her up," Lisa explained.

Lisa's self-loathing deepened and she swallowed another lump threatening to close over her throat.

"Oh, Mason, how could I have let this happen? What was I thinking?"

But she knew exactly what she'd been thinking. She'd been thinking about herself, her own selfish concerns. She hadn't given Katie a moment's thought until she'd heard her call out.

"Why don't you go to Aunt Lisa, and I'll bring your grandma into the house for lunch," Mason said to Katie, giving Lisa a comforting smile.

Lisa was grateful to see him acting as if everything was normal. Yet nothing was normal when it came to her and children…and it never would be. After two years as a pediatric nurse, she still couldn't be trusted with a child. Her carelessness could have caused a tragic accident, and all because she was preoccupied with her own life.

Just like the time she'd been left to care for Linda Jean Bemrose, and a phone call from a friend had distracted her. And to think she'd seriously considered the promotion to head nurse. How could she be responsible for a nursing unit full of sick children if she couldn't care for one healthy little girl?

With a sinking heart, she wrapped Katie in a towel and carried her into the house. Peter was at the table and the minute Katie saw him she smiled and wriggled out of Lisa's arms.

Drying herself with the abandoned towel, legs shaking, Lisa sat down hard in one of the chairs at the kitchen table. Katie climbed into the one chair opposite her and began to eat her lunch as if nothing had happened.

A few minutes later, Mason wheeled her mother in, the two of them chatting in a relaxed, natural way.

"I see they're playing together happily," he said, nodding toward Katie and Peter.

"Yeah, it's as if nothing happened."

"Kids recover quickly," he explained, his expression understanding.

She felt Mason's eyes on her as he moved around the table to the counter. "Anyone for a chicken salad sandwich?" he asked.

She shook her head. Food was out of the question.

As though in slow motion, Lisa got up from the chair and headed toward the living room, guilt weighing down every step. As she passed Mason, he reached out, pulling her into his arms and hugging her against his chest. "Go easy on yourself," he whispered into her hair.

She clung to him, sobs shaking her body. "I feel… so bad," she said.

"Don't. It's over and no harm was done."

MASON FINISHED LUNCH and cleared the table. The children were playing with blocks on the floor next to Carolyn, and she smiled up at him when he came back to stand beside her.

"Are you okay here?" he asked.

"Absolutely." She nodded to the door that Lisa had passed through. "But she's not. Find her. She needs you."

Before leaving the kitchen, he checked to be sure the sliding doors to the patio were locked.

"Daddy, what are you doing?" Peter asked, his tiny face alight with interest.

"I'm going to see Lisa for a moment. You and Katie play and I'll be back," he said, wishing that life was as simple for adults as it was for children.

He found Lisa on the sofa in the living room, her head back, eyes closed. The gray sweat pants and T-shirt she'd changed into emphasized the paleness of her skin. Tears glistened on her cheeks. "How are you doing?"

She sat up and gave him a wan smile. "Not good. Mason, how could I have done that? Leaving the sliding glass doors open that way?"

He eased onto the sofa beside her and pulled her into his arms. "Lisa, children Katie's age need constant supervision, something that every parent learns, but it's new for you. We should all have been more aware of where Katie was, so this isn't just your mistake—it's ours. But regardless, we all make mistakes, and you acted quickly," he said, rubbing her shoulders, feeling the tension in her muscles.

Sitting this close and soothing Lisa's anxiety filled him with longing. A longing based on his need to protect her from harm, to erase all the fear and negative emotions her mother had instilled in her.

"How could I have made the same mistake?" she asked, raising her face to his, her tears cutting straight to his heart.

"What same mistake? Caring for a child is different from any other responsibility. Besides, you've always done your very best by everyone in your life."

She moved out of his arms and sat with her hands listlessly in her lap. "Don't you remember? One time when I was babysitting—the only time actually—the child I was watching had a seizure. I was talking on the phone with a girlfriend, and Linda Jean was playing on the floor next to my chair. The next thing I knew she was flailing around... I called the ambulance and got her to the hospital. But her parents never really forgave me. I couldn't forgive myself, either. For a long time I believed that if I'd been paying more attention to her instead of talking on the phone, I might have..."

He did remember her telling him about that incident, but she hadn't seemed so concerned... Or maybe he hadn't been paying enough attention. "Might have done what?"

She bit her lip in concentration. "I'll never know for sure what I might have done if I'd noticed what was going on before the seizure started. And that's what hurts most—not knowing."

"Lisa, every kid who babysits talks on the phone."

"But I should've been focusing on Linda Jean. She was my responsibility."

"Do you think you could have prevented the seizure?"

"At the time, I was convinced that I could have, but when I was training to be a nurse, I learned that I probably couldn't have," she said tentatively, her anxious gaze meeting his.

"Did she have a medical condition?"

"Not that I knew about, but that's been part of the problem for me. Her parents never spoke to me again, and I didn't dare ask. I wanted to put it behind me. Dad told me not to worry about it. Mom got upset every time the subject came up."

"Did they ask Linda Jean's parents about the seizures?"

"Not that I know of…" Her voice trailed off.

"And all these years you've lived with the belief that somehow you might have caused a little girl to have a seizure."

"Yes, I felt guilty," she murmured.

Hearing the raw pain in her tone, he reached for her, but she moved away. "Mason, this is why I'll never make it as a mother."

"Of course you will. You have. Stop beating yourself up about this. It's over, and everyone's okay," he said, trying for a positive note in his voice to counter the uncertainty in her eyes.

Ever so slowly, she gave him a tiny smile, and he smiled back, his spirits lifting. This time she didn't resist when he tucked her body close to his, her warmth mingling with his.

"Lisa, you told me a little bit about Linda Jean before, but you never explained how that experience affected your feelings toward children. Why not?"

"Because I...I wanted to put an end to my past—move on. I thought I'd gotten over my lack of confidence."

"Until I pushed you on the issue."

"Yeah. Our breakup made me realize that my fear was holding me back, so I took the job in pediatrics to try to overcome it."

"Lisa, why didn't you trust me? If I'd known what the incident with Linda Jean had done to your self-esteem, it might have changed things."

"I guess maybe because of how guilty I felt. How inadequate. Looking back, I realize I assumed it was my problem to deal with."

With complete remorse he remembered what he'd said that night at dinner—how she didn't care about children. What had ever made him say that? Why hadn't he sensed what was behind her decision? "Go on."

"After the night with Linda Jean Bemrose, my mother didn't encourage me to babysit again, and I wouldn't have been willing to do it, anyway. I was too afraid. And that fear only got worse."

"But you must've realized that at some point children would be part of our relationship."

She sat up, moved to the edge of the sofa and gave him a thoughtful gaze. "After feeling inadequate for so long, I simply wasn't prepared to think of my life with a child in it."

So that explained the look on her face the night he'd brought it up. "Lisa, we all have issues that spring from mistakes we've made. I've got quite a list, actually," he said dryly.

She didn't speak or look at him for several moments, and when she did, the misery on her face made him wish he could say the right words to soothe her.

"Lisa, no one's perfect, nothing in life is perfect. And there was no way you could've known that little girl would have a seizure. And what happened a few minutes ago was an accident. Accidents happen to the best of parents."

He clasped her shoulders. "And you're a good, loving parent to Katie," he said.

"Those are words I never thought I'd hear," she said.

As she relaxed into his embrace, his heart swelled in his chest. "This time you're going to stay."

A smile eased the anxiety from her face. "Right here?"

"In my arms," he said, and they grinned at each other.

Holding Lisa close, letting his relief wash over him, he was startled to discover that, for him, loving Lisa had been about how well she fit into his arms— and his life. But he'd taken her for granted; he saw that clearly now.

He'd simply assumed that because she was so easy to be around, that what *he* wanted, *she'd* want. Lisa was the kind of woman who lived to bring happiness to others—her family, her friends, her patients and, at one time, him.

And the saddest truth of all was that he'd never appreciated that caring. If he'd been more aware of her feelings, he would have noticed how reluctant she was to be around children. He could have really listened when she'd told him about her experience with Linda Jean and been there to help her over her fear.

Instead, he'd rushed headlong into his plans for marriage and family, assuming she'd be a willing part of it.

His idea of loving Lisa had been about what *he* wanted, not about what *she* needed. He'd assumed that whatever he saw as important to their relationship, she would agree with because she loved him.

As he felt her body pressed to his, he realized a life without Lisa was out of the question. On the heels of that realization came the unalterable truth. He hadn't loved her the way she needed to be loved.

Lisa deserved a man who'd be there for her...*only* for her.

Ashamed at how little he'd understood her, and how shallow that had made his love for her, he decided that things between them would be different from now on. Whatever it took, he would make it up to her.

"Lisa, I'm sorry for walking out that night. I should have stayed and listened to you. What I did was wrong, and I want to make it right."

She didn't move, nor did she respond.

And when he felt her arms loosen around his body as she edged away from him, he wished he'd never said a word. Her withdrawal reminded him that the last time he'd said what was in his heart, she'd rejected him.

CHAPTER ELEVEN

IF ONLY HE'D SAID *those words five years ago,* she thought.

"Mason, I'm sorry, too, but does that change anything?"

"It might, if we worked at it."

Could she say what was really on her mind? For months after he'd walked out of the restaurant, she'd waited, hopeful that he felt as bad as she did about what happened. She'd even rehearsed what she'd say, that she loved him but she needed time to come to terms with the idea of having children. But he didn't call, and doubt crept in. The day her mother told her that Mason had married Sara she'd been forced to face reality. He didn't share her feelings.

In the midst of what had just happened with Katie, he'd chosen *now* to say he'd talk about it? "You're timing's not great."

He chuckled. "It never was."

Seeing him now, the anxious way he rubbed his forehead, made her wish she wasn't so stressed out. If they were alone and she was more relaxed, talking over their problems would be easier. But when it came to Mason, talking seemed to be the one thing they didn't do well. "Even if we could—I mean, if we had that conversation—it won't change the fact that you may have to move to L.A."

"What if we discover that we still love each other?"

"Then you'd have to choose between Peter and me."

"You really believe that?"

"Yes, I'm sorry. Our lives have changed, we both have family commitments we can't ignore."

She heard Katie calling out for her. "I've got to go and check on Katie."

"Katie's fine with your mother. We need to finish this."

How could she discuss something so emotionally charged with him when she was already anxious about Katie? Besides if she couldn't give Katie adequate care and attention, being a parent herself was out of the question, which meant so was a relationship with Mason.

"I know how much we both need to discuss this, but after what happened with Katie, I need to be with her, to recover a little. Can we do this another time?" she said, getting up off the sofa.

"Whenever you're ready, I'll be waiting."

"Thanks," she said, heading for the kitchen and away from the disappointed look he gave her.

She found her mother sitting with Katie on her lap,

her arms around the little girl. "I think she needs a nap," her mother said. Lisa saw Peter was already asleep in front of the TV. "She also needs you to hold her."

"I want to hold her, too," Lisa whispered, gathering Katie into her embrace. The way her tiny arms slid around her neck, the sweet scent of her skin, made everything seem right again. "You'll be okay with Peter? He looks like he's out."

Her mother nodded and she took Katie up the stairs. In the bedroom, Lisa removed Katie's damp swimsuit and found a pair of Dora the Explorer pajamas for her.

"I'm sorry, sweetie. I should never have left you alone like that. I won't do it again, I promise," she said as Katie raised her arms, allowing Lisa to pull the pajama top over her head.

"I want Mommy," Katie whispered, slipping her thumb into her mouth.

Recognizing the pout of Katie's lips as the warning of tears to come—and unable to handle any more tears—she gathered Katie close to her.

What would she do the day Anne Marie came for Katie? How would she feel when these little arms no longer sought her caring?

As she stood holding Katie, Mason appeared behind her.

"Peter's sound asleep."

Giving him a tentative smile over Katie's curls, she whispered, "I'm hoping she'll fall asleep, too."

Mason eased the rocking chair toward her. "Why don't you sit here for a little while?"

Lisa settled into the chair with Katie cuddled against her, providing her with a feeling of connection, of being essential to this child.

Unwilling to move Katie to her crib until she was asleep, Lisa rocked her gently. "I wish I could erase what I've done."

"Lisa, let it go and enjoy your time with Katie," he murmured.

"But I wanted everything to be perfect!" she protested.

Katie's breath caught, and for a few seconds Lisa feared that her sudden outburst had woken her. When the little girl gave a quick, shuddering sigh and nestled closer, Lisa patted her back to soothe her.

"Lisa, parenting didn't come easily for me, either. Not at first."

"Why? You love children. You were raised in a big family."

"That's true. Still, as much as I wanted children, I had no inkling of what it meant to be a father. Like you, I felt insecure."

"You? But you're a natural with children. Your nieces and nephews love you," she said, trying to make sense of his words.

"What I'm trying to say is that everyone has doubts

about being a parent. Yet despite those early misgivings, after the first couple of months, my feelings for Peter changed."

"How?"

"I couldn't picture my life without him—simple as that. Suddenly there was a living, breathing little person who was not only a part of me, but a part of my life forever. That's what loving a child does to you. You can no longer separate yourself from your child, emotionally or mentally. There's nothing I wouldn't do for Peter."

The vulnerable look in his eyes told Lisa how much he meant those words. The kind of words that spelled the end of any hope for their life together. He would move to L.A. for Peter's sake. A hollow feeling spread from her stomach to her chest; her body tensed, and Katie stirred in her arms.

"You're so lucky, Mason," she said, frantically searching for something, anything, to fill the void forming in her. Until this moment she never really believed that Mason would leave Durham...would leave her.

"I am, and Peter made me see just how good my life's been."

Without me, she wanted to add.

As she rose to put Katie in her crib, Lisa faced the truth. She still loved Mason...would always love him. And worse, at this moment she felt closer to

Mason than she ever had in all the time they were together.

But she still needed to hear his explanation of that awful night, the night he left her. Maybe too many changes had taken place for them to find common ground on which to begin again, to believe in themselves as a couple with a future, but she needed to hear him say the words.

"Lisa, why don't you come downstairs with your mother and me?" he asked, putting his arm around her shoulders. "I'm sure Carolyn's worried about you."

"I…I should stay here for a bit, in case she wakes up. I'm afraid she'll be upset, and I don't want that. I need her to understand she's safe with me…. Somehow she has to see—"

"Lisa, if you cling to her, you'll make her think that something's wrong. It's perfectly normal for her to have a nap after lunch. Stick to her routine, don't encourage her fear."

"The way my mother would have, is that what you're saying?"

"Let me take her," he said. Gently Mason eased Katie out of her arms, his gaze never leaving Lisa's face as he moved to place the sleeping child in the crib.

Lisa watched, acutely aware of how happy and contented she felt in this room with Mason beside her. "Isn't she adorable?" Lisa whispered, her heart flooding with love for the little girl.

Mason rested his hands on Lisa's shoulders, and the warm touch of his skin on hers made her want to put her arms around him and never let go.

"She is. And she's also loved, all because of you," he said, bending his head close to hers.

Slowly he lowered his lips to hers, his arms sliding around her.

She closed her eyes and answered his kiss, feeling the strength of his body beneath her fingertips.

As his lips covered hers, all the worry that had haunted her slipped away, leaving her feeling newly fulfilled.

"Mason, thank you," she whispered against his lips. His powerful hands encircled her waist as he pulled her deeper into his embrace.

"You don't have to thank me," he said, speaking softly next to her ear, making her body shiver with excitement. He held her face in his hands, his hungry eyes sweeping her features. She could feel his heart beating a tattoo beneath her fingers.

"Daddy?" Peter's still sleepy voice broke into the moment.

Mason grinned as he turned to his son standing in the doorway. "What is it?"

"Why did you kiss her?" Peter asked.

He hugged Lisa close, burying his face in her neck. "Because I want to," he said.

CHAPTER TWELVE

THE NEXT DAY Lisa and her mother sat in the sunroom recovering from their latest shopping spree. They'd bought Carolyn new clothes and knitting supplies so her mother could return to her old hobby.

And all the while, Lisa couldn't erase the feeling of Mason's lips on hers.

True, a kiss between friends was wonderful, but Mason's kiss had not been that of a friend.

"I'm really looking forward to my session on Monday with the physiotherapist. And I'm going to start a sweater for Katie." Her mother gave a contented sigh. "You and I always seem to have a great time, no matter what we're doing."

"We do, don't we?"

She was just about to get up to put coffee and cinnamon rolls on the table when the phone rang. When she answered, she was delighted to hear Anne Marie's voice.

After a moment of casual exchanges over the weather and what their mother had been doing, Anne Marie switched topics. "Where's my precious angel?"

she asked, her voice overflowing with excitement. "Mommy has news."

"She's watching *SpongeBob* on TV, her thumb in her mouth and her arms wrapped around Nemo," Lisa replied.

"Sounds like she's having fun. Can you tell her that Mommy wants to talk to her?"

"Sure." Lisa went and got Katie.

"Mommy!" Katie squealed when she heard her mother's voice. She hugged the phone close to her face. "When are you coming?" she murmured, her tiny lips kissing the phone, her eyes lit up with joy.

Lisa witnessed Katie's delight at hearing her mother's voice, her excited giggles spreading happiness around the room.

"Mommy wants you," Katie said, passing the phone to Lisa while she climbed into her lap.

"Hello again," Lisa said, making room on her lap for Katie, gratified to see the pleasure on her niece's face.

"Boy, it's great to hear Katie. And I have wonderful news. I've been released! All the charges are dropped."

"You're kidding! What happened?"

"Just a couple of days ago, after the investigator you hired did some checking around, the police found a huge stash of marijuana and oxycontin in a storage locker rented by Jeff. His prints were all over the packages. Then one of his accomplices agreed to give evidence in exchange for a lesser sentence. Jeff confessed—and not only that, he told the police I wasn't involved. I was so relieved! Mr. Watt says they have no direct evidence linking me to Jeff's operations, and I was being used as a cover."

"Fantastic! Mom," she called over her shoulder, "they've dropped the charges."

Hugging Katie tight, she passed the phone to her mother and listened as Carolyn talked excitedly, her face suffused with happiness.

Lisa's throat tightened at the realization that her family had a chance to be together. Having Anne Marie in Durham would be wonderful; she was sure her sister would take her offer to live here while she found a job and an apartment.

"Anne Marie wants to speak to you again," her mother said, her eyes bright with unshed tears.

"Anne Marie, I'm so excited for you."

"Well, if it hadn't been for that lawyer and the investigator you hired, I'd still be locked up. Thanks, Lisa."

"You're welcome. We can't wait for you to come to Durham! We want you to stay at the house with us while you decide what you're going to do next. I know there are tons of job opportunities in Durham for you, or you could go back to school."

"As a matter of fact, that's what I wanted to talk to you about. While I was waiting to be released, I had lots of time to think about my situation, and I've decided that I'm going to become a social worker. I'm sure it sounds like a huge project to take on, and I'll be tight for money—"

"You don't have to worry about money. You've got me."

"Lisa, you're the best sister I could ever ask for, but I don't want you paying my bills."

"At least stay here while you go back to school."

There was a pause. "This will probably sound strange to you, but things changed for me while I was in jail."

"I can see how that could happen," Lisa said enthusiastically.

"I met a social worker who helped me see how lucky I was to have been given a second chance to make a life for myself and Katie. There are a lot of women here in Florida without an education, little or no family support or financial means. I was one of them. With the aid of others—and you—I survived. Now I want to help these women restart their lives. The social worker is going to put my name forward to an organization that gives educational funds to women in need, like me."

Lisa hardly dared breathe at the implication of Anne Marie's words. "Does that mean you'll leave Katie with us while you go back to school?" she asked hopefully.

"No, I need Katie and she needs me. I'm coming up to Durham on Monday to get her—and to visit with you and Mom. I can't wait to tell you all about my plans."

It was as if the bottom had fallen out of Lisa's life. "Mom and I are more than willing to help you in any way we can, and that includes keeping Katie at least until you're settled in your school program."

"Lisa, I love you for saying that, and believe me, I would cherish the idea of having my family near me. I'll talk to you about the possibilities when I get there. In the meantime, kiss my daughter for me, will you?"

"A roomful of kisses coming right up," Lisa said, hugging Katie even tighter while she did her best to hide the leaden feeling crushing her heart.

MASON PLUNKED THE PHONE down again, half relieved and half frustrated that Lisa's line was still busy. He'd decided last night to talk to her about his plans for the future, maybe get her input, work on finding out how she felt about him now. The situation between them had gone on long enough.

Holding Lisa for those few moments last night made him happier than he'd been in a long while, but was that enough?

It hadn't been when they were together, or they wouldn't have broken up. Maybe the busy phone offered a good excuse for him to reconsider his idea of talking to her today.

Still, maybe now, before he chickened out, was

the best time to call. He reached for the phone, then changed his mind.

Hell, he hadn't felt this indecisive in years. All his life, he'd taken charge, made decisions—usually because someone had to do it. But deep down he knew it was because he *liked* making decisions, a trait that served him well as a police officer, where the ability to take charge could mean the difference between life and death.

Resigned that he wouldn't be able to get any work done as long as he continued to debate with himself, he dialed her number one more time.

When she answered, her voice was thick, as if she'd been crying. "Is everything all right?" he asked, expecting her to cover, to say that things were fine. Lisa was an expert at avoiding her feelings.

"Mason, Anne Marie called and she's been cleared of all charges."

"That's great news!"

"It is," she said, and this time he could hear a distinct sob in her voice.

He glanced around his office, looking for his car keys, ready to race over to her house. "Lisa, what's wrong?"

"I'm sure you're busy, but can you come over? I don't mean to impose, but I'd really appreciate you being here."

How long had he waited to hear those words?

And how pleased he was to hear them. "I'll be right there."

Clipping his cell phone to his belt, he got in the car and drove across town to Lisa's house.

He could see her at the back door when he pulled into the driveway, her face drawn and anxious. "Thanks for coming so quickly," she said, relief evident in her voice.

Despite her emotional state and red-rimmed eyes, she had never looked better to him.

"What can I do?" he asked, putting his arm protectively around her shoulders.

"I need...to talk to you," she said, glancing behind her. "Mom has Katie with her, so let's go into the living room."

They settled on the sofa, his arm moving immediately to the cushion behind her shoulders. He was acutely aware of how much he'd like to hold her while she cried, and offer her every bit of advice he could think of.

But he held back, keeping in mind his promise to let her work her problems through and wait until she asked for his help.

"Mason, Anne Marie will be here on Monday to get Katie and take her back to Florida," she said, her words rushing past her lips.

He whistled in surprise. "Take Katie?"

"Now that she's been released, she has a whole

new life plan," Lisa said as she explained what had gone on, her words hurried.

"I thought Anne Marie was going to come here to live."

"I did, too, but she's not. She's going to school in Florida, and she wants Katie with her." Lisa clutched the edge of the sofa.

"I'm not ready to let her go. I tried to talk Anne Marie into staying with us while she goes back to school, but she's made plans to go to college in Florida to become a social worker. She wants to help other women in trouble."

"Lisa, unfortunately, there's nothing you can do about this other than to be happy that you gave Katie a good home and lots of love. For a few weeks you were Katie's mom. I'm proud of you."

Her fingers squeezed his arm. "But I don't get it. Why wouldn't she want to live with us?"

"Anne Marie probably wants to do this on her own, and she's to be commended for it. Given where she was in her life when you met her, she's made a lot of progress in putting things back together." He turned to her. "That doesn't help you very much, I realize."

"Not really... I guess that's a bright spot, when you look at it that way," she said, a small smile lifting the corner of her lips. "Can I assume she's done something to impress you?"

"You may. Not many people survive what she has

and come out with a commitment to help others—usually it's the other way around. But right now, I wish there was something I could do to ease your concerns about Katie," he said, letting his arm slip around her shoulders.

She leaned into his embrace, nestling her head into his shoulder, and Mason's heart picked up speed.

"What am I going to do? I love Katie. She means the world to me. I never thought I'd feel like this about a child. Now that I do, I'm going to lose her."

Mason scrambled to think of all the things he could say. He could tell her that this was a risk she'd taken from the beginning, that Katie belonged with her mother, that life often isn't fair.

But none of that mattered.

Slowly and gently he pulled her against him, and as he did, he felt her sudden intake of breath followed by racking sobs.

He'd never seen Lisa cry like this in all the years he'd known her. As he held her close, the truth stared him in the face.

She'd never trusted him enough to let him see her fall apart. Yet she did now. She was part of his life once more, and he wanted to keep it that way. He wanted to be with her when Anne Marie arrived to get Katie.

In the past, she'd accused him of being too controlling, too quick to take charge of any situation. But one fact was crystal clear. If he was ever going to have a second chance with Lisa, he had to respect her need to work things out for herself.

If Lisa wanted him here when Anne Marie came, she'd say so. Until then, all he could do was hold her and comfort her. She needed a friend right now, and she'd chosen to confide in him. He'd be content with that.

They sat together for a while longer, neither making a move. Gradually he could feel Lisa relax in his arms....

He relished this moment of complete quiet with her as she rested against him.

After a few minutes, she sat up, smoothed her hair and faced him. "I must look awful. I'm going upstairs to wash my face."

He met her tearful gaze, searching for the right words. "You're beautiful. You're always beautiful," he said, his heart in every syllable.

"Thank you. It's nice of you to say that, but I've seen what I look like when I cry." She touched his cheek, a lingering touch that made him want to make love to her, right there on her couch in broad daylight with her mother only a few feet away in another room.

To get his thoughts off Lisa's body, he decided to go to the sunroom with Carolyn while Lisa went upstairs. He discovered Katie in the midst of piling all her stuffed animals into her grandmother's lap.

"How's Lisa?" she asked, the expression on her face one of concern.

"She's having a rough time."

"I'm so glad you could be here for her. She relies on you for so much. If I may be so nosy, what went wrong between the two of you?"

"Did Lisa tell you anything?" he asked, surprised at the blunt question, so unlike anything Alice would have done.

"No, but I can see how you behave around each other. You both have feelings for each other. Lisa is a wonderful woman who's taken life entirely too seriously. I'd like her to relax and have more fun. I just don't know how to get her to do it, but I thought maybe you might."

He was tempted to say what was on his mind, but his feelings for Lisa were too raw.

Weeks ago, he'd believed that he was over her. But the past few days had proven just how big a fool he'd been on that front. But loving Lisa would require patience and caring and, most of all, his respect for her ability to make a life for herself.

If Lisa wanted her mother to learn about her past, she had to be the one to tell her. "Lisa is a very complex, very special woman."

"There you are," Lisa said as she came into the sunroom, a smile planted on her face and all traces of tears wiped clean.

The determination in her movements and the set

of her shoulders told him Lisa was back in control. "I have to get going," he murmured.

"I understand," she said, walking with him to the door. "We'll be in touch," she said, the old Lisa firmly in place.

The urgent way she'd needed him only an hour ago was completely removed from her face and her behavior. Would Lisa ever be free to feel things without the pressure to contain those feelings? He didn't have a clue, but he hoped that, with Carolyn Lewis's support, Lisa might learn to handle her emotions differently.

Or was he simply waiting for the moment when she would trust him again?

"Sure. You know where to reach me."

As MASON WALKED to his car, Lisa blocked the urge to call him back—a desire so powerful it frightened her. She needed him in her life; without him she felt adrift in an uncertain world.

He'd been waiting for her to confide in him, but she couldn't. That would make her open to the pain of losing him when he moved away.

And he surely would, if his life with Peter was at stake.

She couldn't face losing anyone else.

Confused and tired, she returned to the sunroom to talk to her mother.

Carolyn stopped her knitting, glancing up at Lisa.

"Honey, Mason is a wonderful man. Do you want to tell me what went wrong between you?"

At first, she was taken aback by her mother's open approach. Then she saw the love in Carolyn's expression, and felt an urgent need to share what had happened.

"Mason and I loved each other, but when he asked me to marry him, he made it conditional on having children. I wasn't prepared to make that kind of commitment. I was…afraid."

"Oh, Lisa. Is that why you went into pediatrics?" she asked astutely.

"Well…yes."

"Every parent has anxieties around raising a child. Heavens, I'm hardly a stellar example of being a mother," she said to the click and clack of her needles. "I was never at ease with Anne Marie, and I think she sensed it. I often wonder…if I'd been a better mother, maybe Anne Marie would never have taken up with that useless bum."

"Does Anne Marie know how you feel?"

"No, I haven't got the courage to tell her, and what good would it do? But thanks to you, Anne Marie's turning her life around."

"Mom, that's something I want to talk to you about. I have the money, and I'd like to pay for Anne Marie's education and help with day care for Katie. We could also have them come up here on school breaks and summer holidays," Lisa said, her spirits lifting as she thought of opportunities to see Katie again.

"I'm glad to hear you say that. We can work on this. After all, keeping our family together as much as possible is important. And it *is* our family, isn't it, dear?"

Her mother's words lingered, echoing in her heart, making her feel valued. She could still play a big part in her sister's and Katie's life, and have a special relationship with her mother.

Hearing her mother's words, she suddenly felt as if she were really home...really and truly part of a family. Mason had wanted a family with her. She'd refused to consider it, but now she realized what a family with children meant to her. Katie had made her happy, had shown her what love for a child could do...what she had given up.

CHAPTER THIRTEEN

BUT BY MONDAY WHEN Anne Marie arrived at the door, Lisa was again fighting her old insecurities about being left out as she watched Katie race into her mother's arms.

"Oh, sweetie, I'm so glad to see you," Anne Marie said, kissing her daughter and hugging her close.

Trying to ease her sense of loss, Lisa concentrated on what it meant for Katie to have her mother back. "Katie really missed you."

"Not nearly as much as I missed her," Anne Marie said between kisses, accompanied by Katie's squeals of laughter.

The love between Anne Marie and Katie was so clear, so filled with joy, Lisa found herself wishing for a moment like this in her life. "Yeah, Mom and I had a wonderful time playing with her. She's so easy to care for, and we enjoyed every minute."

Resting Katie on her hip, Anne Marie hugged Lisa. "I'm sure I sound like a broken record, but I truly appreciate your support. I have no idea what I would've done without it."

"That's what families do for one another."

As she hugged her sister back, Lisa felt the stirring of need for a child of her own. The thought made her heart pound, and she tightened her arms around her sister. What if she did want a child of her own? Was it real, this sudden need, or was she looking for a child to replace Katie? She stepped out of her sister's embrace, tucking her arms close to her sides.

Anne Marie turned to her mother as they entered the kitchen. "Mom, it's great to see you, and you look so much better. Living here obviously agrees with you."

Anne Marie hugged her mother next and sat in the chair beside her at the table. Lisa poured coffee all around while Anne Marie held Katie on her lap and told them about her plans.

"This may seem like a fantasy idea, especially for someone with no postsecondary education and no money, but I've never felt more determined in my life. It's as if I've been given another chance to make good—not just for me but for other women who have lived as I have. The difference is that I was saved from my fate by my sister, and I want to be a sister to some of these women."

"That's wonderful, Anne Marie," her mother said, her face animated.

Feeling the loss of Katie, yet pleased for her sister, Lisa sat down across from Anne Marie. "Yeah, Mom and I talked it over. You can come here anytime, leave Katie with us whenever you need to, and I'll help you with your college expenses."

Anne Marie shifted uncomfortably. "I don't want charity. You've already paid big bucks for a lawyer, and I won't be able to repay you for a long time. I've made a lot of stupid financial decisions."

"My adoptive parents left me with enough money to do pretty much as I please. That doesn't mean I'm going to leave nursing, but it does mean I can afford to offer you any financial assistance you need. I'm so grateful to have you in my life." She touched Katie's hands where they rested on Anne Marie's. "And I'm grateful for getting a chance to look after Katie."

A whirlwind of thoughts spun through her head, but the one that wouldn't go away was the idea of having a baby. She knew only too well how over-whelmed she felt when it came to children, but caring for Katie had added a whole new dimension to her life. And had given her the courage to consider having a child of her own.

Suddenly close to tears, Lisa got up from the table. "What about lunch? I've got sandwiches and salad ready."

"That would be great, but then I have to get on the road. I wish I could stay longer but I have to be back in Florida to get all my courses set up. I promise Katie and I'll be back for a visit as soon as humanly possible," Anne Marie said, easing Katie off her lap and standing. "Let me pour Katie's juice," she said, giving Lisa another hug.

Lisa listened to more of Anne Marie's excited talk about her plans, but she couldn't eat a bite. All she could think about was that, in a few minutes, Katie would be off to Florida. Sure, she'd see her again, but it wouldn't be the same.

After lunch, she helped Anne Marie load Katie's things into her car, her anxiety building as their good-byes drew nearer.

Lisa had just closed Anne Marie's trunk and was about to follow her into the house when the sound of a car pulling up at the curb caught her attention.

Climbing out of his car, Mason closed the door and started toward her. She had never been so glad to see anyone in her life.

"How's it going?" he asked her, his long strides bringing him quickly to her side.

She tried to mask her relief at seeing him standing there, his look of concern telling her he was aware of how emotionally drained she was feeling. "Katie leaves in a few minutes."

"I figured as much. I'm here for you." He touched her hand, his fingers encircling hers in his powerful grip.

She wanted to wrap her arms around his neck, tell him how much she needed to keep Katie with her and to be part of the little girl's life on a daily basis, but no words came.

Instead, she squeezed his hand.

THE ACHE HE SAW in Lisa's eyes made him want to take her in his arms and hold her while she cried, but the stiffness of her shoulders showed her determination not to let anyone know how upset she was.

"When she goes, I want you to take me up on my offer of dinner tonight," he murmured close to her ear.

"I didn't know you'd made one," she responded, the tension easing from her face as a smile quivered at the corners of her mouth.

"Will you go out to dinner with me? I do have to go to a party at my parents later, but you could come as my date. We'll dress up, and I'll even wash my car." He nodded in the general direction of his coveted Corvette.

"You wash your car every day, but you never invite me to parties," she teased, relief visible on her face.

Although he suspected she might be anxious about seeing his family again, Mason felt unreasonably pleased that he could make her smile under the circumstances. "I wash it every *other* day, but today's will be a thorough scrub-down, all for my best girl," he said and then could have kicked himself.

That had been his nickname for her when they were together. With four sisters and three nieces, he'd kidded Lisa that calling her his "best girl" put her at the top of his list.

"Are you reminding me of better times?"

She glanced toward her back door as Anne Marie came out carrying Katie.

"We said our goodbyes to Mom," Anne Marie said, passing Katie to Lisa. "Hi, Mason. It's good to finally meet you."

"You, too. And congratulations on your release."

"Thank you for all your help. Lisa's lucky to have you in her life."

While they chatted, Katie squirmed in Lisa's arms as she smiled up at Mason. "Read me a story?" she asked.

"Sometime soon. I'll read you a whole bunch of stories," he said, watching Lisa's face for her response.

Lisa chewed her lip as she held Katie close. "We'll have lots of chances to read stories when you come to visit again."

Without looking at Mason, she took Katie to the car, and put her in her car seat. "We'll see you soon, Katie, I promise. In the meantime, you take care of your mommy, and we'll talk on the phone every day. Okay?" she asked as she fastened Katie into the seat.

"Thanks again, Lisa. For everything. Come visit us in Florida on your vacation. I'm hoping the police will let me back into my house soon, but for now I've rented the house next to Cindy's," Anne Marie said, hugging her sister.

The way Lisa clung to Anne Marie tightened Mason's gut. As the car moved down the driveway and turned onto the street, Mason moved closer to Lisa, his arm automatically going around her shoulders.

"They'll be fine," he said, attempting to console her.

"I won't," she said, putting her arms around his waist and squeezing him so hard he could barely breathe.

LISA HAD ALMOST canceled their dinner date. She'd been so emotionally and mentally exhausted after Anne Marie left that all she wanted to do was go to bed. But seeing Mason sitting across from her now—dressed up in a suit, no less—made her glad she'd kept the date.

Although their conversation had been a little stiff so far this evening, he seemed to be enjoying himself. She was, too. She also appreciated the time away from her thoughts of Katie's departure and its impact.

The waitress appeared at the table, her full attention on Mason. "Will there be anything else?" she asked, her smile inviting.

Mason didn't seem to notice as he took the check and tucked it next to his napkin. With dinner nearly over, disappointment made her anxious. Mason hadn't said one word about them as a couple, or anything very personal.

"This has been so pleasant, and I've had a nice evening," she said, smiling at him as the waitress brought more coffee.

"So have I. One of the nicest in a long time, actually," Mason said as he shifted in his seat, and rested one hand on the table. "I just landed a major new client, so it looks like Stephens Investigations will live to see another week."

"Congratulations! That's terrific news. And it was a smart move to change the name of the company."

"Yeah, I needed a new image."

Mason rubbed his jaw, a frown of concentration on his handsome features. "But I had no idea how much tact and interpersonal skills it takes to run a business. It's sure different from being a police officer."

"Are you regretting what you did?"

"No. Although there are challenges, especially the client who expects instant results." He rolled his eyes. "But I enjoy being my own boss. And Tank has been good to me, sending clients my way."

"Tank's been good to both of us," she said, remembering that day in his office. "And I want to thank you again for finding my mother…and Anne Marie."

"And Katie?"

"Yes, Katie most of all. Anne Marie called to say

they were stopping at some friends' in Savannah and would be home tomorrow."

"That's good." He paused. "And, Lisa, I want to apologize for some of the things I said about Anne Marie when we were in Florida. I was wrong. Anne Marie's a decent person who deserves a break in life."

"You were concerned that I was getting involved in something I couldn't handle," she said, looking into his eyes. She was surprised and encouraged by what she saw there—the same vulnerability she'd seen the day he'd comforted her after Katie fell in the pool. A vulnerability he'd never shown when they were dating.

"That's partly true," he said deliberately.

Was he going to say anything about their past? What would she do if he did? A lot had changed between them since that trip to Florida, including how she felt about children being part of her life. For the first time, she wanted them to talk about it, and the thought made her excited, if a little uneasy.

"And?" she asked, hoping he would share more of himself with her.

"Oh, you know, my good old white-knight thing." He smiled ruefully as he played with the knife at the side of his plate. "There's been quite a bit going on in my life the past few months and I've come to see that my take-charge attitude can be more of a hindrance than I realized."

"You? Being introspective?" she asked and could have bitten her tongue when she saw the look of embarrassment on his face. What had made her blurt that out? But Mason questioning his behavior was a new development, and it had taken her by surprise.

In the past, Mason Stephens had never shown much inclination to examine his motives.

HE COULDN'T BLAME Lisa for being a little skeptical of a change in him, especially one like this. He had to admit he'd been pretty determined, not to mention bossy, when they were together.

So far, the evening hadn't gone the way he'd planned. He'd had every intention of easing into the topic of their breakup, but there never seemed to be the right opening in the conversation. The hovering waitress didn't help.

Lisa had talked about Katie, which he enjoyed, but it left little room to move the conversation to any adult discussion. But deep inside, he had to admit that he was reluctant to bring up that night in case he spoiled the intimacy between them.

He and Lisa were getting along well, and he didn't want anything to change that. Remembering his promise to himself to go slow, he said, "Have you decided to take the head nurse's job?"

"I was seriously considering it—until the pool incident. Now I'm not sure if it's a good idea. The position carries a lot of responsibilities."

"Do you believe they would have offered you the job if they weren't certain you could do it?"

She caught her lower lip between her teeth. "You've got a point."

"Then why don't you—" He blocked any further words of advice. Lisa had to make her own decision.

She nodded her head slowly, the beginnings of a smile framing her mouth. "Accept the job? I just might do that."

As he began to organize his thoughts to broach the topic of their breakup, he glanced at his watch. Damn! They were going to be late to his parents' party, and he'd promised his mother he would be on time. "We better go if we want to make the party at my parents'. You're coming, right?"

"Sure. I love your mother, and I want to thank her for the food she sent for the playdate. What's the party for, anyway?"

"My sister Evelyn's leaving for Denver tomorrow. She's got a new job there as head librarian at the city library. She gave up her apartment, and has been staying at Mom and Dad's until she goes. I promised to see her before she left and it turned into a family dinner."

"Mason, do you think this is a good time for me to go to a family party with you?"

"I didn't mention you were coming, but I want you

to be there. I'll explain everything else when we get there. Okay?"

"I don't want to impose," she said, sounding uncertain.

"You won't. Besides Mom was asking about you the other day. She didn't realize that I was working on a case for you."

Lisa's expression softened. "How is your mother?"

"She's fine. Spending her days cooking, bossing Dad, complaining when I don't come and see her. I'm at the top of her 'you don't visit me anymore' list." He caught the eager look in her eyes. "So, what do you say?"

She gave him a lopsided grin. "What's it worth to you?"

"Oh, so this is how we're going to do it," he said jokingly, remembering how they once kidded each other about making things "worthwhile." It had been their way of dealing with the conflicting schedules of Lisa's nursing career and his police duties. "Okay, let's see. I'll trade you one thirty-minute visit with Mom and Dad for one afternoon of staying with your mother when you need it. Do we have a deal?"

She slipped her purse strap over her arm. "What are we waiting for?"

WHEN THEY REACHED Mason's parents' house, Lisa accompanied him into the kitchen where everyone was laughing and waiting to dig into a late-night meal of fried chicken.

"Mom, you're the best cook around, but we just had dinner," Mason said in response to his mother's request that they have something to eat.

"Who's with you? Sara?" his father, Leonard, asked, entering the kitchen from the den. "Oh, hi, Lisa." He glanced at Mason, then back at her. "Good to see you."

"It's nice to see you, too," Lisa said, feeling awkward as the various Stephens siblings and their families greeted her, while the unspoken question of what she was doing here with Mason hung in the air.

"Evelyn's upstairs finishing her packing. She said she wanted to see you as soon as you got here," Leonard informed Mason before sitting down to the huge plate of chicken his wife had placed on the table. This seemed to be the cue for everyone else to follow suit, talking loudly among themselves as they did.

"I'll go up and see her. Is that okay with you, Lisa?"

"Of course. I'll talk to your mom," she said, raising her voice over the convivial din.

Mason disappeared upstairs while Lisa took the chair beside Leonard and enjoyed the lively conversation about the latest antics of the Duke Blue Devils. Finally Mason's mother joined them.

"I was sorry to hear about your mother," Mary Stephens said, sitting next to her.

"Thank you," Lisa said. "I miss her."

Mary placed her hand on Lisa's. "How are you doing?"

"Not bad. I've been pretty busy getting my mother—my birth mother—settled at my house," Lisa said, and everyone at the table stopped talking and fixed their collective gaze on her.

She glanced around uncomfortably. "Mason helped me find my mother in Florida—and, as it turned out, my sister and niece, too."

"Yes, Mason mentioned he'd been working with you. He hasn't told us much about it, though," Leonard said, his voice controlled.

If her pleasure at finding her family meant anything to Mason, why hadn't he mentioned it to someone in his family? And why had Leonard assumed that it would be Sara with Mason? A hard ache started behind her heart and spread through her chest.

Feeling totally alone and hurt, she did her best to make conversation until Mason reappeared.

But by the time he did rejoin her, it was getting late. "I need to get home. Mom's waiting for me," she said, keeping her tone neutral.

They drove in silence through the city, a silence Lisa found harder and harder to bear. The reaction of the Stephens family toward her had been awkward, leaving her feeling like an outsider. A distinct change from when she'd been dating Mason and the Stephens house was her second home. She missed feeling part of his family, the closeness, the warmth, being included.

"You're very quiet," he said as he swung the Corvette into her driveway.

"Why hadn't you told your family about my mother and sister, and why did your father expect Sara to be with you?"

He hesitated. "Lisa, my life has been chaotic lately, too. Dad's not the easiest person to talk to, even under the best of circumstances," he said, shutting off the engine.

As they sat in the darkened car, she pushed for an answer. "So, why didn't you tell them my good news? They may not be part of my life anymore, but I thought you'd want them to know I was happy."

Mason tightened his grip on the steering wheel as a deep sigh rushed past his lips. "Lisa, I haven't had an opportunity to visit my parents in weeks because I've been busy at work. As for Dad, he's worried about what'll happen to Peter if Sara goes through with her plans. In Dad's mind, a child is worth doing whatever it takes to keep both parents under the same roof. When he realized I had a woman with me, he probably just assumed Sara and I had been out somewhere together."

He reached over and took her hands, pulling her toward him. "Please don't go looking for what isn't there where Sara and I are concerned."

"But obviously your parents are holding out hope

for the two of you," she said, annoyed with herself and angry at him for how the visit to his family had made her feel.

"Sara is out of my life—except as the mother of my son." He looked directly at her. "I want to be with you. I'll let my parents know about us when the time is right. Tonight was too chaotic, I'm sorry."

"You want to be with me even after everything that's happened over the past couple of years?" she couldn't help asking.

"Lisa, we need to work out what's going on between us—the sooner, the better. I know you have to get back to your mother right now, but I'd like to see you tomorrow night," he said, his voice low, his body way too close to hers.

Why did it bother her so much that Mason hadn't told his family about her changed circumstances? Why did what his family knew about her life suddenly matter?

Mason leaned toward her and kissed her lips before she had a chance to respond, a kiss that lit the need burning inside her.

Starved for him, she drew him to her, sliding her fingers over his shirt. Urged on by his intake of breath, she returned his kiss.

"When we do talk, I hope it starts off like this," he said, settling back in his seat.

Caught in a vortex of need, she couldn't match his light bantering tone, so she said nothing. In the silence of the car, she fought to control the thudding of her heart, her burning desire. Mason was the only man she wanted, but wanting someone wasn't always enough.

"I'll walk you to the door."

With the taste of him still on her lips, she slipped the key in the lock and went inside.

CHAPTER FOURTEEN

"A PENNY FOR YOUR thoughts, dear," her mother said as she wheeled into the kitchen where Lisa sat staring at the newspaper the next morning.

"Oh, Mom, my thoughts aren't worth much."

"Would I be right if I guessed either Mason or Katie?"

She sighed and smiled at her mother. "Both, actually."

Her mother wheeled her chair next to Lisa. "Please don't worry about Katie. Anne Marie is a good mother, and Cindy will be looking after Katie while Anne Marie is in her classes. I'm more concerned about you."

"Me?"

"Dear, I hope you don't feel I'm a busybody, but how are you doing?"

Aware that her mother was scrutinizing her pretty closely, she sat up straight in her chair. "I'm fine."

"How was your date with Mason last night?"

"The dinner was lovely. Afterward, we went over to his parents' house. His sister Evelyn is moving to

Denver," she said, keeping her eyes on the cup of coffee she passed to her mother.

"Did you enjoy yourself?"

"I did." She didn't want to involve her mother in this right now.

"Then, honey, why the long face?"

She sighed in resignation—apparently her mother *did* want to be involved. "Because nothing seems to be working out the way it should."

"Between you and Mason?"

Taking a sip of her coffee, she put the cup down. "We're never on the same page. It seems that whenever we get a chance to talk, we don't. It's my fault as well as his, but if one of us doesn't open up soon, it may be too late."

"I'd like to lock you two in a room until you talk this all out. But let me tell you something about your dad."

Lisa nodded, placing the newspaper on the counter.

"Your father was the warmest, most affectionate man in the world, and I always felt so cared for when he was around. Everyone who met him loved him."

"You weren't just a little biased?" Lisa teased, awed by how her mother described her father.

"I certainly am. Grant worked with the local power utility, and he would often pay the bill for a family in need rather than see their power shut off."

"He must have been a very kind man."

"He was. Your father had this incredible ability to make me feel special, even when we argued. We didn't argue all that often—mostly we worked things out."

Lisa sighed. "I wish it could be the same where Mason and I are concerned."

"Lisa, love isn't the same for everyone. We all have our own story. What's yours?"

"I don't really have a story, Mom. I loved Mason from the moment we met, and I wanted us to be a couple. Then one day he asked me to marry him, and I was ecstatic, and things were perfect—or so I believed." She winced. "Then Mason insisted that we discuss a timeline for having a family. But it was less of a discussion and more of a dictation. I didn't have any say in the matter. Back then I couldn't see myself as a mother, and to be honest even if he had agreed to wait, I wouldn't have considered it."

"Why not? You were a great mother to Katie."

"I was never happier than when Katie was here with me." A knot twisted in her stomach. "But it wasn't always that way...."

She explained about Linda Jean, and how, when she'd tried to tell Mason, he hadn't taken her anxiety seriously.

"If Mason loved me enough to want to marry me, why didn't he understand the effect that Linda Jean's seizure had on me?"

"Maybe being from a big family meant he'd seen

a lot of mishaps involving his siblings, or maybe he was accident-prone himself. Maybe he thought you were telling him because you were over your fear."

"Over it? I'm not sure I'm over it now. I went into pediatrics after we broke up to prove to myself that I could care for a child, in the hope that I could conquer my anxieties."

"And now there's the head nurse position."

"Yes, I have to decide if I'm going to accept it soon."

"I think you should. You love children. I know you have doubts, but I'm sure this job will make you believe in yourself again. Lisa, darling, you do your best in everything."

"Thanks, Mom. I just wish the rest of my life was working out as well as my professional life."

"Honey, I've watched you and Mason—there's a strong connection between the two of you and I can tell how much you mean to each other. Want my advice?"

"Do I have a choice?" she asked, smiling at her mother's eagerness.

"Don't give up. You and Mason are so well matched. Take a chance on him. What have you got to lose?"

"Everything, if he follows his ex-wife to L.A."

"Did he say he's doing that?" her mother asked, a shocked expression on her face.

"Mason loves Peter so much that he may feel he has no choice but to go."

"Did you and Mason ever talk about why you broke up?"

"No."

"Wasn't that why you went out to dinner last night?"

"Yes."

Her mother smiled sadly. "So both of you sat there, avoiding the one topic you needed to broach.... How awful."

"I just couldn't tell him how I felt without a little encouragement from him. I didn't get any." Lisa shrugged.

Her mother pushed her coffee cup aside. "Do you love Mason? Don't stop to think about it, just answer."

"Yes, but…"

"No buts. The very next opportunity, you tell Mason what you just told me. That you want to try again, and see what he says. Now I won't pressure you any more about it."

Yes, she loved Mason despite everything that had happened in the past few years. She loved him and her mother was right. She needed to tell him everything, including the revelation that she would like a family…with him.

"Thanks, Mom, for everything."

"If you don't mind changing the subject, I've been

meaning to ask if you have any photo albums of when you were young. I only ever had the one picture, and I'd like to see more."

"The attic is filled with memorabilia. Why don't I go see what I can find, and you and I can spend the afternoon going over them," she said. Looking forward to more time with her mother, Lisa went to the attic.

UP IN THE ATTIC, with the smell of old wood surrounding her, she felt some peace return. The attic had been her playroom when she was a kid. But the last time she'd been up here was after her dad passed away, and then only to put a box of his papers in storage.

Peering around in the low light, she spotted her old high chair and a pink chest of drawers on which her collection of antique dolls rested.

Back in the corner were dozens of boxes of photos from her childhood. Here, amidst all these things Alice Clarke had saved, she felt her love more than in any other part of the house.

Someday she'd go through everything hidden away in all the nooks and crannies, but for today she had to decide which of the photo boxes to take downstairs.

She was rooting through the boxes when she heard someone on the steps. "Who is it?" she called out.

"Me." Mason's head appeared over the floor-boards.

Her heart jumped in anticipation. They were alone up here; this was her chance to say everything that had been on her mind. "Hey. What's up?"

"I came by to see you," he said, making his way to where she stood.

His smile was so tender and inviting she wanted to slip into his arms. "I'm looking for photos of me as a child to show Mom. Funny, I've been talking a lot about family lately," she said, searching for the right words.

He moved closer, and she could see that he'd nicked his chin shaving that morning.

"You'll have a full day going through all this stuff."

"Mom wants to know all about me, and I want to hear more about my dad."

"Old photos are one of the nicest ways for you and your mother to share your lives," he said, his hand coming to rest on her shoulder, his smile tentative.

Her skin warmed beneath his fingers, and she couldn't stop herself from leaning into his touch. "But the very best part of this for me is that I don't feel left out anymore. I'm part of a family. And I understand why you wanted one of your own now. I think…I want that, too."

He looked shocked, then his eyes widened in plea-sure. Her breath caught in her throat as she watched his mouth, wishing he'd say something, or simply kiss her. Without thinking, she licked her lips, her head tilting back.

The scent of his soap and his skin enveloped her as his gaze held hers. "Oh, Lisa…" he whispered as he edged closer, his lips just above hers.

She slid her arms around his neck and pulled him down to her. Coming alive at his touch, she kissed his chin and his throat, as her fingers clasped his gold chain. The urgent pressure of his body against hers fueled her desire. Her mouth met his in a hot, passionate kiss, bringing her alive to his touch, to her need for his love.

His breath coming in short gasps, he eased away from her, his eyes filled with longing. "Honey, you have some timing. I actually came here to tell you something."

She opened her mouth to speak, but he pressed his fingers over her lips.

"It's final. Sara *is* moving to California and taking Peter with her," he said, a tremor in his voice.

"Oh, Mason, I'm so sorry. You love Peter. You're such a great dad. What will you do?"

"I'm not sure. If I stay here, I'm afraid Peter won't understand why I'm not with him, so I feel I have to be there when he needs me. But if I go, I'll be leaving you and I'll have to start over with no support from my family. Sara wants it both ways—a new career on the other side of the country *and* our son. How can she possibly think that moving Peter is a good thing?"

Crushed by the raw pain in his voice, she put her arms around him. "Mason, is there anything I can do?"

"At this point, I don't know what anyone can do. I talked to Sara about leaving Peter with me, but she wouldn't agree."

"Can't she see that Peter will lose out on so much without his family near him?"

"Sara's not too concerned about family," he said ruefully, his own arms tightening around her.

Whatever it took, she'd help him, ease his pain.

Holding him close, she murmured, "Mason, what's next? Where do we go from here?"

"Damned if I know, but I've got to find a way…" he replied. His arms fell away from her. The pain was gone from his eyes, replaced by a preoccupied stare. "I've got to go," he said abruptly. "I'll call you later."

"But—"

He turned from her and strode across the floor to the steps.

He was leaving. While she was trying to support him through this, he was walking away from her and what she was offering.

At the top of the steps, he spun back to face her, dragging his fingers through his hair, a habit so familiar it made her want to cry.

"I'm sorry, Lisa, but I need to work this out for myself."

Surprise and hurt jolted her. "So much for starting over," she whispered over the thud of his feet moving down the wooden stairs.

He was going it alone, she thought bitterly. He'd never included her as an equal partner in their relationship, never shared all the ordinary problems of life. He always had to be in charge, get his own way, no matter how much it hurt anyone else—including her.

Mason clearly hadn't changed. He expected to make the decisions and she was expected to go along with them.

The one time she hadn't, he'd walked out on her.

Now that she was offering to share in the decisions, he'd left—again.

MASON HATED HIMSELF for the pain he'd seen in Lisa's eyes, but he couldn't help himself. He couldn't help much of anything today. The prospect of losing his son had knocked him for a loop. He'd been well aware that this could happen, but he hadn't truly believed it. What a fool he'd been.

He'd never felt this vulnerable. This sense that his life was out of his control was foreign. Frightening.

He needed to come up with a plan or be relegated to seeing his son a few weeks a year.

Those few weeks wouldn't allow him to be a real

father. But was moving to L.A. logical if he had no one to support him?

Yet the one person whose support he craved, he'd walked out on. He wanted to retrace his steps, go back to Lisa and make up for his behavior. He loved her, not just because she was such a kind person—as he knew from experience—but because she made every part of his world work.

When they were together, she'd cared for his friends, listened to his stories and told him hers. She was always there to cheer him on, tease him when he got too serious, get him to laugh when life showed its ridiculous side. And now they wanted the same things—home, family. But the cost would be his relationship with Peter.

And he might have already screwed things up between him and Lisa. The hurt look on her face a few moments ago said he'd made a serious mistake by turning away.

He'd done it again.

Dammit! Why hadn't he let her be involved? There was probably nothing she could do, but she'd been willing to try, and he'd shut her out.

And all this time he'd believed that she was shutting *him* out, not paying attention to him. But she had been completely open and focused on him, and he'd walked away without a word of explanation.

He should've stayed in the attic, listened to her

suggestions and let her caring ease his sense of losing control.

But the truth was, he didn't know how to ask for help. He'd always been the one people leaned on. And he'd grown up in a policeman's house where being in charge was as natural as breathing.

Except that now when *he* needed someone to lean on, he couldn't find the words to ask, to admit that he was afraid and lonely.

And now he stood to lose the one woman who mattered most to him.

CHAPTER FIFTEEN

THE FOLLOWING MONDAY, Lisa pulled into the hospital parking lot, ready to start her first day as head nurse of pediatrics.

Mason's behavior last week had shown her that he wasn't nearly as serious about their relationship as she was, that in a crisis, he didn't need her. She shuddered at the thought of how close she'd come to telling him she loved him.

In the aftermath of his abrupt departure, she'd decided to focus on her career and accept the promotion. She'd had a very positive meeting with the VP of nursing last Thursday and came away feeling upbeat and ready to do the job.

Being head nurse would effectively remove her from direct patient care, but on the other hand, it would give her a chance to be involved in planning for the unit and perhaps making some changes.

On the way up the elevator to the fourth floor, Lisa decided that she'd have a meeting as soon as possible to get feedback from the staff on some of her ideas. She felt fairly confident that the other nurses would be receptive; she'd worked with all of them at some point in her normal nursing rotation and had a good relationship with them.

Having been away, she didn't expect to know any of the patients on the unit, but she planned to sit in on the morning report to bring her up to speed. Eager to get to her new job, she hurried down the corridor toward her office, which was just inside the doors of the unit.

She entered her office to find a huge bouquet of roses on her desk. "Wow! Who would have done this?"

She put her purse in the cupboard behind the desk, and picked the card out from among the roses. Mason's name was scribbled on the small white square of paper, but nothing else.

She hadn't heard from him since their conversation in the attic. She'd wanted to call him but couldn't because she didn't know where she fit in his life. The fact that he hadn't called her had been painful, but obviously Mason had his own priorities. She simply wasn't one of them. "I'll call him later today and thank him." She hoped she got voice mail, though, as she wasn't prepared to have a conversation that made her feel even lonelier than she did now.

"Good morning, head lady. The pressures of the new job making you talk to yourself already?" Melanie said from the doorway.

"Good morning to you, too. And no, I'm just admiring the roses."

"Those arrived a few minutes ago from Mason. I peeked at the card. They're beautiful, aren't they?"

"They are." Mason had sent her flowers to welcome her on her first day back—and starting her new job. She was touched by his kindness.

"I wonder how he knew I was starting today. I didn't tell him."

"You didn't have to. I told him. He and Sara have been here since the night before last. Peter was admitted to Emergency. He had an appendectomy."

"Oh, no!" What a frightening thing for any little boy, but knowing him made it more personal. Only days earlier Peter and Katie had played together, his sweet nature so endearing, so easy to love. "Is he okay?"

"He's fine, and so cute. Of course, being his aunt makes me a little biased."

"Why didn't someone call me?" Why hadn't *Mason* called her? He'd know she'd be concerned.

"I assumed Mason would've told you, although he and Sara have been here, staying with Peter around the clock. I've gone to check on them every chance I could get, and I've never seen my sister so upset. She and Mason have certainly come together to deal with this crisis. It's nice to see them like that."

"I guess so..."

Mason and Sara working together to care for their child. And why not? They both loved him. It wasn't unusual for parents to put aside their differences for the sake of their child. Did that explain why Mason hadn't called in a week? Had he and Sara reconciled?

After being a surrogate mom to Katie, she could say with certainty that if she were in their situation, nothing would keep her away from her child. Why would Mason be any different? He loved Peter and she finally understood how powerful that love could be.

"Mason's with him now, making sure he eats a bit of breakfast. Peter is being discharged tomorrow."

"I hope he'll be okay. Peter and Sara are supposed to be leaving for L.A. pretty soon, aren't they?"

Melanie shrugged. "I haven't asked. They haven't wanted to talk about their plans, but I'm sure Sara will give me an update when this is over. But I've got to get going now—duty calls. I just came by to officially congratulate you."

"Thanks. I'll talk to you later," Lisa said, her mind on Mason and how hard this must've been.

He'd obviously been too worried about Peter to call. She felt selfish that she'd only been thinking of herself. She'd drop by the room and see if she could do anything. And if Sara was there, she'd offer her sympathy, now that she understood with her heart as well as her head how a mother would feel.

At the nurses' station, she checked the room number for Peter, then went down the corridor. The door was closed, making her hesitate for a moment. Mason had probably closed it because Peter was asleep.

She quietly eased the door open and peeked in. As she'd expected, Peter was asleep.

Silhouetted against the light from the window, Mason and Sara stood next to his bed, their arms wrapped around each other. Mason's lips were pressed to Sara's forehead, his arms cradling her.

Shock tumbled through every part of Lisa's body. Embarrassment made her cheeks flare hot. Desperate to obliterate the look of happiness on Sara's face, Lisa closed her eyes.

Her fingers trembling against the cool surface, she carefully shut the door.

"WHO WAS THAT?" Sara asked, stepping out of Mason's arms as she glanced toward the slowly closing door.

He wanted to swear. "Lisa," he said.

"She saw us? Like this?"

He'd seen the devastation on Lisa's face and had no doubt that she'd jumped to all the wrong conclusions. "Look, can you stay for a few more minutes and watch Peter? I need to find Lisa and tell her what's going on."

Sara nodded. "Sure, but I have to be back at the house in an hour."

"I won't be long."

Of all the rotten luck! He was sure Lisa had assumed the worst where he was concerned and he could hardly blame her. Why hadn't he taken the time to call her, tell her what had happened with Peter? She would have been so understanding and caring... But he realized that after he'd left her in the attic, he didn't know how to ask her to forgive what he had done.

He hurried down the corridor to Lisa's office while he mentally prepared what he'd say to her. When he got there, she was at her desk reading a document, her blond hair tightly confined at the back of her head. She looked all business—just as he'd expected.

"Can I speak to you for a minute?"

She glanced up, her eyes clouded, her face pale. "Certainly. I trust Peter's doing well," she said, the formality in her voice negating any familiarity between them.

"He's fine and ready to go home tomorrow. But I came here to talk about something else."

"Thank you for the roses. They're lovely," she said, pulling her chair closer to her desk.

"Roses seemed appropriate, given your accomplishment. Congratulations, by the way."

"Thank you." She placed her hands firmly on the desk and locked her eyes on them. "What did you need to see me about?"

"I'm sorry I haven't been in touch for the past few days."

"That's completely understandable, given the circumstances. You don't have to apologize."

Lisa had the ability to seem calm and cool regardless of how she felt inside. Today of all days, he wished she'd let her real feelings show so they could both deal with them. "I think I do. This wasn't how I wanted this conversation to go."

"Meaning what?" She shifted her gaze to him.

That gaze held agony, embarassment and remorse in equal measure, and he was responsible for all of it. For a few moments he could think of nothing to say that would change what he saw in her eyes. Feeling set adrift by the emotions of the past few days and the distance forming between him and the woman he loved, he managed to dredge up the words, "Meaning, what you saw in there wasn't what it looked like."

HOW SHE HATED being a cliché. The woman who misunderstood a man's intentions and assumed—incorrectly—that he was interested in her. There was no explanation that would make what she'd seen any different than what it was.

"Mason, as you've said before, we're friends. As a friend, I'm relieved that Peter's all right. As a friend, I'm happy you have the life you want, whatever that is."

Her heart battering her chest, she clasped her hands tighter and waited for him to leave. She couldn't let herself cry in front of him, and somehow she had to get through her first day.

"Lisa, Peter's illness has changed everything between Sara and me. We've talked a lot these past few days about what's best for him. We've finally come to a decision—"

She put her hands up to stop his next words, words that would confirm her fears. "This isn't the time or place to discuss your personal life. I realize that's a little harsh, but I have to get back to work."

She needed to get him out of her office before the tears gathering in her eyes fell over her cheeks. All her dreams had died when she'd opened that door, and she couldn't stand the thought of learning the details of Mason's new life without her.

It was natural to conclude that Peter's illness would bring Mason and Sara together again and that now they'd move out west as a family. That was all Lisa could bear to know.

"I'm sorry. Don't give up on me," he said, exhaustion evident in his words. But he wasn't the only one who was exhausted. She was tired of all the effort it took to work out their relationship, to discover a way for them to get back together. Yet all along she'd known he'd never leave his son. She'd wasted so much time and effort on a man who had told her from the beginning what his first priority would always be. When she didn't respond, he turned and walked away.

LISA MANAGED TO GET through the rest of her shift. That night she slept fitfully, dreaming that Mason and Sara were in her house, their lips moving, but she couldn't hear a word they said.

When she went into work the next morning, her head ached so much she wanted to go back home. She couldn't. She had an important meeting with nursing management over staff changes.

When she got to her office, there was a note that Sara Campbell had asked to speak with her. She rubbed her arms to ward off the apprehension. She wanted to see the woman about as much as she wanted to meet a snake. She could ignore the message, but she had to admit to a certain amount of curiosity about the woman Mason had married.

Grudgingly, she went down to Peter's room, this time opening the door quickly. If she had to witness Sara and Mason in an embrace again, she'd be better prepared.

But all she saw was Sara holding a sleeping Peter in her lap while an older woman looked on, obviously Peter's grandmother.

"Good morning. I'm Lisa Clarke. You wanted to speak to me?" she asked, pleased that her voice sounded authoritative, yet friendly.

"Hi, Lisa. This is my mom, Madeline."

"It's nice to meet you," she said politely.

"I've wanted to talk to you for a long time. That day Mason introduced us in the grocery store was rather awkward. He often speaks of you," Sara said, her expression open.

What could she say? After yesterday, Lisa had no reason to concern herself with who or what they talked about.

"I'm glad Peter's doing well enough that you can take him home today."

"Yes, you just caught us. We were almost ready to leave," Sara said, giving her mother a quick smile as she passed Peter to her.

Madeline eased the child onto her shoulder, one hand on his back, holding him protectively. "I'm going to take Peter down to the car. Your dad is wait-ing for us," Madeline reminded Sara, adjusting Peter against her shoulder.

"Thanks, Mom. I'll be along in a few minutes." The other woman nodded and walked out of the room.

"He's a great little boy," Lisa said, meaning every word. "When do you leave for L.A.?"

"On Friday. I can't believe it. I've waited all my life for this opportunity, and I'm not going to pass it up, regardless of what people think. This is my big chance," she said, the smile on her face triumphant.

How could the woman be so excited about a change that could take Peter away from his father? Melanie had remarked on how concerned Sara had been about Peter when he was sick, and now all Sara could talk about was her career.

"What did you want to see me about?" Lisa asked.

Sara smoothed her auburn hair as she gazed out the window. Turning back, her hands on her hips, she began.

"Lisa, you and I aren't friends, and it may not be my place to say this…" She shrugged. "Or my business."

Then don't. She didn't want to hear any more, but any good excuse for walking out seemed to have abandoned her.

"I think you should stop being so stubborn. Mason said he tried to explain that you misunderstood what you saw yesterday, but you refused to listen."

What was there to misunderstand? She hadn't heard from Mason in days and then she walked in on their intimate moment. She was tired of feeling left out when it came to Mason, his life and his family. Now this woman had the gall to think that she was in a position to offer advice to Lisa. Obviously Mason and Sara had talked about her, and the thought made Lisa angry. What right did either of them have to meddle in her affairs? They had their lives all neatly worked out, and that made them an authority on hers? Not likely.

"That's none of your business," Lisa said, anger snapping through her.

Sara frowned. "Have you spoken to Mason since yesterday?"

"No, I haven't," she admitted.

"You should," she said, plucking her sunglasses out of her hair and planting them on her nose. She picked up her purse and left the room.

RELIEVED TO BE HOME, Lisa showered and started dinner, letting the familiar routine soothe her anxiety.

"How's Peter doing?" her mother asked, wheeling her chair around the kitchen with a dexterity that had been absent a few days ago.

"He was released this morning."

"Oh, that's good. Why don't you look happy?" she asked, a concerned expression on her face.

"I met his mother, Sara. As far as I know, she's taking Peter to L.A. with her as soon as the doctor gives the okay."

"And how does Mason feel about that?"

"I'm not exactly sure," she hedged, not wanting to go into the details. "The last time I spoke to him about it, he was very upset."

"And now you know he'll have to follow them."

Hearing her fear put into words unnerved Lisa. What she'd seen in the hospital confirmed that Mason was leaving with Sara, yet a part of her couldn't believe it. How could Mason let her think he wanted more of a relationship with *her* if he was going away?

"I honestly don't know if he'll go or not. Mason made it clear that he didn't need my help or advice."

And now she understood why. As Peter's illness had shown, in a crisis Mason turned to Sara. Those stressful days must have convinced him that, for Peter's sake as well as his own, he should move with Sara.

"Oh, honey, that's awful! You two don't seem to be able to connect. Anybody with eyes can see that you care for each other."

"I think you're misreading this situation, Mom," Lisa said.

"Sit down here for a moment." She patted the chair next to her at the table. "What can I do?"

"Unless you can create miracles or cast spells... nothing." Lisa sank down into the chair.

"Did he say anything to you in the hospital?"

If she could erase the few minutes she'd spent with Mason yesterday, she would. She'd never felt worse in her life than when he'd walked into her office, wanting to discuss his plans.

"Mason was there to be with his son, not to talk to me," Lisa responded a little too sharply.

"Okay," her mother said soothingly. "I want you to listen. Years ago, your father and I had a fight. It didn't start out big, just one of those disagreements all couples have about how to discipline a child—in this case, Anne Marie."

Lisa's adoptive parents had never argued in front of her, but she'd learned very early in life that the sound of crying behind her parents' bedroom door meant trouble. "What did you do? Were you unhappy?"

"At the time, but every marriage has those moments when both the husband and wife wonder what ever made them believe the relationship could work. And like everyone else, I got out my list of grievances I'd been harboring for months. How your father didn't listen to me. How he left Anne Marie's care to me, and now he was questioning what I did."

Her mother's expression turned sad. "But most of all, I was afraid that given our financial circumstances, your father was upset that I was pregnant again. We didn't have the money for a second child, and the best I could hope for was an entry-level job when I did go back to work."

"Was he upset about me?" Lisa asked, worried now that she might have been a source of friction between her parents.

"No, of course not. I was having the usual emotional ups and downs created by hormones. Still, we fought and he wouldn't back down from his opinion that I was spoiling your sister. I was so angry. I walked out and went to my sister-in-law's. But I soon regretted my foolish mistake. I knew that if your father and I were going to get past our differences, we needed to talk them out."

"What did you do?"

"I left Anne Marie at your aunt Helen's house, swallowed my pride and went home. And I'm so glad I did because your father was leaving to take a course in Tampa the next day. If I hadn't gone back, I would never have been able to say how sorry I was for the stupid argument."

"Then what happened?"

"We made up and he invited me to go with him to Tampa. I arranged for Anne Marie to stay with Helen and we left that night, feeling closer than we had since we were first married," she said, her voice low, her eyes fixed on some distant point.

"We were still talking when the eighteen-wheeler crossed the median and plowed into us."

"Oh, Mom, I'm so sorry. Why didn't you tell me this before?" Lisa asked.

Carolyn smiled at Lisa, her face alight with love. "I thought it would be too painful for you after losing your mom, and I didn't want to cause you any more sadness. I realize now that you need to understand something very important before it's too late."

Feeling her mother's love, Lisa took her hand. "What's that?"

"If we hadn't listened to each other, if we'd let our anger and fear of rejection rule our relationship, I would've been hiding out at Helen's house during the last few hours your father lived. Can you imagine how horrible it would've been to face the guilt of knowing that I allowed my pride to stand in the way of making up with Grant?"

Lisa was speechless at how easily the outcome between her parents could have been so different, if her mother had not gone home to her father.

"You must have been very thankful for the chance to spend those last hours with Dad."

"It wasn't simply chance. I made the conscious decision to do whatever I could to keep our marriage strong. If I'd been stubborn, I would have regretted it."

"I hope I can do that when the time comes," Lisa said wistfully.

"But, Lisa, that's the whole point. The time *has* come for you and Mason. When are you going to swallow that pride of yours and talk to him?"

CHAPTER SIXTEEN

HER MOTHER'S WORDS still echoing in her head, Lisa drove across town to Mason's house, only to realize that he might not be there. She pulled over to the curb and called him on her cell. He answered immediately, and she felt silly about being so impetuous.

You'd better get this right, it's your last chance.

"Mason, it's me, Lisa," she said, gripping the phone with one hand while she steadied the other on the wheel.

"Hey, it's good to hear from you. Everything all right?"

He sounded distracted, but she had to say the words before she lost her courage. "Can I come over? Is this a bad time?"

"No. In fact I was going to call you. I want to explain what you saw in the hospital and apologize for not calling you, but my life has been insane. There's so much I need to tell you."

He had things to tell *her?* Lisa was very proud of herself for the way she had taken control over her own life recently, and she didn't want to lose that—even for Mason. If they were to have any kind of relationship, he had to understand that they were equals. What she wanted was every bit as important as what he wanted. "I want to talk to you, too." She closed the phone, thrilled at feeling in control of the situation. Now that he'd agreed to meet, what was she going to say? How should she begin? Should she wait for him to speak first? No! She was the one taking the initiative, and she would have her say.

Lisa pulled back into the traffic and was on Mason's street a few minutes later—just in time to see Sara leave Mason's driveway.

What was Sara doing here?

But why *wouldn't* she be there if they were back together?

The memory of their embrace flashed across her mind. Letting the engine idle, she clenched the wheel, trying to steady her thoughts.

It had all seemed so simple a moment ago, before she'd seen Sara leaving Mason's house. But now, doubt creeped in, and she felt utterly alone. What was *she* doing here?

Had Mason sent Sara away so he could talk to Lisa, give them a little privacy while he broke the news?

He'd probably told Sara that he owed Lisa an explanation, and that he hadn't managed to give it to her at the hospital. Meanwhile she'd come all the way across town to blurt out her feelings for him.

Her determination of a few minutes ago flowed

out of her on a wave of mortification. What a fool she'd been! Why had she been so impulsive?

You promised Mom you'd talk to Mason.

Her mother had faith in her, loved her and wanted the best for her. That was why she'd encouraged Lisa to talk to Mason. She breathed deeply, remembering her mother's courage all these years—*her* courage. She was her mother's daughter and she could do this. She clamped her lips together and squeezed the wheel even tighter. Damn! Mason *did* owe her an explanation.

She barely had the car door open when Mason came striding across the lawn, a hesitant smile on his face. "Come on in the house," he said, beckoning her toward the back door. "I'm glad you came."

Lisa's heart beat faster and her determination wavered, but remembering her mother's words, she followed him inside.

As soon as she entered the house, she could hear *SpongeBob* on the TV and Peter's delighted laughter.

"Want a cup of coffee? I made a fresh pot," he said as she closed the door.

"That would be nice," she said through dry lips.

Near the end of the kitchen counter she could see several packed bags and a collection of toys.

"Have a seat and I'll find some food. Might even scare up a cranberry muffin, just for you."

Muffins? How could he talk about muffins one minute and tell her was leaving the next?

"Are you having one?" she asked, an odd squeak in her voice as she stared at him.

"If you are. There's not much else in the house."

No food in the house usually meant somebody wasn't planning to be there very long. Her stomach roiled.

"Was that Sara leaving as I drove up?" she asked as she scrambled to find a way out of her misery. She couldn't sit here and drink coffee as if nothing had changed. He obviously planned to move to L.A. Otherwise, why all the suitcases and the empty fridge?

Would he have told her he was leaving if she hadn't called? Had her phone call reminded him that he wanted to give her some sort of explanation? She'd never know for sure now, but one thing was clear. Faced with the reality of his packed bags and devotion to Peter, she couldn't tell him that she loved him. She had to get out of this house.

"You need to be with Peter before he…before the flight to L.A."

Feeling humiliated, she turned to the door, anxious to reach the safety of her car.

"Lisa, wait! What's going on?" he asked, striding across the kitchen. Taking her by the shoulders, he turned her around, forcing her to face him.

"Look, I have news," he said, "but I also need your advice. Why don't you and I sit down in the living room and talk? Peter will be fine. Nothing distracts him from *SpongeBob*."

Mason's smile warmed the space around her and yet…it sent her heart plummeting. He'd never asked for her advice before, except maybe about the choice of tie or what shirt to wear.

"Why do you need my advice?"

"Peter's going to be very upset by the move, and I saw how well you handled Katie when she was lonely. How can I make this easier for him?"

CHAPTER SEVENTEEN

WHAT WAS HE SAYING? Why would Peter be upset if both Mason and Sara were going to be with him?

"I don't understand..."

Sighing, he tilted her chin up, his dark eyes studying her. "As usual, this isn't coming out right." He sighed again. "Lisa, I'm not going to L.A. with Sara."

"You're not?"

"Sara finally agreed that the best place for Peter is here with me and my family. That's what I was trying to tell you that day in your office."

Lisa gulped in embarrassment. "So you and Peter are staying here in Durham?"

"It sure looks that way," he said.

Relief made her giddy. "Why didn't you *tell* me?" she asked, easing out of his reach while she straightened her thoughts. If Mason wasn't going away with Sara, life suddenly had possibilities.

"I knew when you saw Sara and me in Peter's room, you assumed I was moving to L.A. and that I was getting back together with her. But you wouldn't give me a chance to tell you the truth."

Feeling her cheeks grow hot, she turned away. "What was I supposed to believe? You told me that you'd do anything for Peter."

"But I wouldn't try to resurrect things with Sara. I was hugging her because she'd just agreed to leave Peter here with me."

"That's...nice." Taken completely by surprise, those two inadequate words were the only ones she could come up with.

He slid his arms around Lisa's shoulders, holding her close. "When Sara told me she was definitely moving, I learned what it was like to lose control. I was terrified that my son would grow up without me, and I'd end up being on the margins of his life. I couldn't stand that, but I didn't want to leave you, either. Strange as it may seem, Peter's illness was a blessing. It forced Sara to realize that if anything happened to Peter out in California, she'd have no one to rely on. She also recognized—finally—that Peter needed the love and support his family gave him here in Durham."

She could see the truth in his eyes, a truth that swept away all her uncertainty. "And I walked in while you were hugging each other and jumped to the wrong conclusion." She shook her head. "How easily mistakes are made in a relationship."

She slipped her arms around his waist, seeking his warmth. "After you left the attic and didn't call,

I assumed you'd decided to move to L.A. rather than lose Peter."

"Did you really believe I'd make that kind of decision without talking it over with you? I love you. I couldn't leave you, and I couldn't let Peter go without me. My whole life was crashing around me."

"I didn't have much faith in us, did I?"

"I didn't give you much reason to believe we had a future."

"How did two smart people like us get it so wrong?" she asked.

"And I should have trusted you that night five years ago, listened to what you had to say. We might have ended up differently. It wasn't until I watched you with Katie, and saw how well you handled such a huge change in your life, that I began to understand that I needed to take stock of *my* life and how I lived it."

"What does that mean?"

"That I woke up and realized what was right in front of me." His smile started in his eyes before edging down to his lips.

A wave of happiness rose through her, leaving her breathless.

Lisa wanted to curl up in his arms. She wanted to believe they could compromise, accept their differences and move on *with* each other.

Mason ran his fingers along her jaw. "When I think of all the times after we split up when I wanted to call you, even for coffee… But I know now, that if I had tried, I would've failed. I'll never see you as just a friend."

"Being friends was your idea, remember?"

He grimaced. "Bad idea."

A strange fluttering rose in her chest. "Because you don't want to be friends."

"I want us to start over from the beginning. Is that okay with you?"

"That might work." The words came out weak, compared to the feelings storming through her.

Gently he led her to the living-room sofa and sat down beside her. Without touching her, he murmured, "I want you in my life. That doesn't sound very romantic, but it's the truth."

She heard the love in his words, and remembered another time, other words of love. Placing her hands on his chest, she whispered, "There's still a voice in my head, the voice telling me not to take risks. But I'm trying not to listen."

"Then don't. Your parents believed they were showing their love for you by encouraging you to play it safe," he said gently.

She nodded. "And I was the perfect, dutiful daughter."

Her body tingled at the feathery touch of his fingers along her cheek.

"But it's not about your parents anymore. It's about you and me and what we want out of life."

"You make it sound so easy. As if I could change by simply snapping my fingers."

"You've already changed, and I'm going to silence that voice once and for all," he told her as his lips replaced his fingers along her cheek, lingering on her heated skin, fueling her need for him.

AFTER SEVERAL MOMENTS, Mason said, "You can't remove all risk from your life, and besides, a little risk is good for the soul." He kissed her lips, enjoying the sound of her tiny gasps that let him know she was feeling the same thing he was.

"I grew up in the original house of mayhem, but never for a minute did I not feel loved."

"I've envied that…a little," she murmured against his throat, her lips hot on his skin, sending his pulse into overdrive.

"Lisa, I learned from my parents that love is about wanting to be with someone so much that you couldn't imagine your world without that person. For me there is no world without you and Peter."

"Are you sure?"

"When I walked out of the restaurant that night after saying all those awful things, what did you think?"

"That you didn't love me enough to hear my side of the story," she murmured, pulling back from him.

Panic welled up in him. He'd faced down criminals and been in many dangerous situations, but none of them had made him feel as exposed as he was now.

This time around, he had to get it right.

He felt the old urge take over. He could easily say she'd misunderstood…put words in her mouth.

He'd done it so often.

"Why don't we talk about it now?" he said.

Finally, after all this time, and one botched trip to the altar, Mason understood that marriage was about the give and take of real equals, and *that,* above all, was what he wanted.

CHAPTER EIGHTEEN

"WHEN WE HAD DINNER that night, I wasn't expecting you to ask me to marry you."

"Why not?"

"Because there were so many things we hadn't discussed, including children."

"For instance?"

"You weren't happy in your job, and I didn't think we were ready for changes in our personal lives until your work life was settled. And I'd been feeling unsure of myself, and now I know why. I wasn't aware of how much I resented you making all the decisions in our relationship. I felt I wasn't being heard, and I couldn't get you to listen. When you left the restaurant that night, I realized that unless something happened to change your attitude, you weren't ever going to really listen to me. It sounds like I'm being too analytical about our relationship..."

"Go on," he said, barely above a whisper, his eyes never leaving her face.

Silence churned between them, heightening her tension. "When you insisted that I agree to the number of children you wanted, I felt completely trapped. I thought you understood that with my mother's anxieties over children and the incident with Linda Jean, considering being a parent wasn't an easy thing for me. I didn't know how to respond."

"And yet when Katie came into your life, you seemed to jump at the chance to be a mommy. That was a little confusing for me."

"Yeah, it was confusing for me, too. I was terrified."

"But you took her in and cared for her despite that fear."

She looked into his eyes, at the love shining there. "I could do it because my family believed in me. I needed to feel I mattered."

"And I didn't make you feel that way?"

She shook her head. "You always jumped in, took charge, and I began to feel inadequate."

"I'll admit I had trouble seeing you as being willing to take charge of a potentially difficult issue. Like your new family—I was worried you were in over your head."

"Tell the truth. You thought I was losing it," she chided.

"You weren't losing it. I know why you did what you did. I guess I was worried, trying to protect you. That's all I was ever trying to do."

She nodded, not sure what to say next.

MASON HAD BEEN avoiding this conversation for five years, but now that they were having it, waiting for Lisa to continue was driving him crazy.

He had vowed he wouldn't break in, but it was taking all his self-control not to.

Instead, he reached to touch a strand of hair that clung to her cheek.

Despite their differences he'd been in love with Lisa from the first day he'd met her.

Why the hell couldn't he simply say that? Indecision wasn't his style. When she didn't say anything else, he leaned forward, resting his arm on the back of the sofa, and took her hand.

"Lisa, I will never again leave you out of a decision, or give you reason to believe I don't value you in every possible way. I can't guarantee that we'll be happy. No one can. What I *can* tell you is that I love you so much. I've made a lot of mistakes where our relationship was concerned, but I don't want to make another one that could jeopardize what we have together," he murmured.

"I don't want to make a mistake, either," she whispered, her gaze on him, her lips moist and inviting. "Oh, Mason, I love you and we can make it work. I'm sure we can," she said eagerly, cuddling closer as she kissed his chin.

He expelled the air from his lungs in one long sigh. He held her, burying his face in her neck. "You can't imagine how long I've waited for this moment, how many times I thought you'd fall in love with someone else before I could find my way back to you."

She held him, her hands in his hair, her breath warm on his neck. "When we met that day in Tank's office, I was worried that you'd see how uncertain I felt, knowing you'd once again be part of my life. It'd been years since I'd spoken to you—I had to rehearse every word I said. I've missed you so much."

He leaned back on the sofa, pulling her against him, luxuriating in the smooth fit of her body against his.

"When Tank called me about your mother's case, I was eager to help you. Truth is, I was riddled with guilt over how I'd behaved that night, and grabbed the chance to make it up to you."

"Can we agree never to let misunderstandings come between us again? I can't go through this twice!" she said, drawing his face to hers.

"Agreed." He tucked her body even closer to his as he kissed her—a long, sweet kiss.

"Although I think our old problems are over."

"Why?"

"Because you and I love each other, we have our careers and our families. But most of all I've learned that a child changes everything."

"Do you mean Katie?" he asked.

"And Peter. And later...*our* child. Yours and mine."

"Our child," he said. "Peter's brother or sister. Katie's cousin."

She smiled as the tears spilled from her eyes.

* * * * *

COMING NEXT MONTH

Available September 14, 2010

LARGER-PRINT BOOKS!
GET 2 FREE LARGER-PRINT NOVELS PLUS
2 FREE GIFTS!

♦HARLEQUIN®

Super Romance

Exciting, emotional, unexpected!

YES! Please send me 2 FREE LARGER-PRINT Harlequin® Superromance® novels and my 2 FREE gifts (gifts are worth about $10). After receiving them, if I don't wish to receive any more books, I can return the shipping statement marked "cancel." If I don't cancel, I will receive 6 brand-new novels every month and be billed just $5.44 per book in the U.S. or $5.99 per book in Canada. That's a saving of at least 13% off the cover price! It's quite a bargain! Shipping and handling is just 50¢ per book.* I understand that accepting the 2 free books and gifts places me under no obligation to buy anything. I can always return a shipment and cancel at any time. Even if I never buy another book from Harlequin, the two free books and gifts are mine to keep forever.

139/339 HDN E5PS

Name	(PLEASE PRINT)	
Address		Apt. #
City	State/Prov.	Zip/Postal Code

Signature (if under 18, a parent or guardian must sign)

Mail to the Harlequin Reader Service:
IN U.S.A.: P.O. Box 1867, Buffalo, NY 14240-1867
IN CANADA: P.O. Box 609, Fort Erie, Ontario L2A 5X3

Not valid for current subscribers to Harlequin Superromance Larger-Print books.

**Are you a current subscriber to Harlequin Superromance books
and want to receive the larger-print edition?
Call 1-800-873-8635 today!**

* Terms and prices subject to change without notice. Prices do not include applicable taxes. N.Y. residents add applicable sales tax. Canadian residents will be charged applicable provincial taxes and GST. Offer not valid in Quebec. This offer is limited to one order per household. All orders subject to approval. Credit or debit balances in a customer's account(s) may be offset by any other outstanding balance owed by or to the customer. Please allow 4 to 6 weeks for delivery. Offer available while quantities last.

Your Privacy: Harlequin Books is committed to protecting your privacy. Our Privacy Policy is available online at www.eHarlequin.com or upon request from the Reader Service. From time to time we make our lists of customers available to reputable third parties who may have a product or service of interest to you. If you would prefer we not share your name and address, please check here. ☐

Help us get it right—We strive for accurate, respectful and relevant communications. To clarify or modify your communication preferences, visit us at www.ReaderService.com/consumerschoice.

HSRLP10R

HARLEQUIN®

A *Romance*

FOR EVERY MOOD™

Spotlight on

Heart & Home

Heartwarming romances
where love can happen
right when you least expect it.

See the next page to enjoy a sneak peek
from Harlequin Superromance®,
a Heart and Home series.

*Enjoy a sneak peek at fan favorite Molly O'Keefe's
Harlequin Superromance miniseries,*
THE NOTORIOUS O'NEILLS, *with
TYLER O'NEILL'S REDEMPTION,
available September 2010
only from Harlequin Superromance.*

Police chief Juliette Tremblant recognized the shape of the man strolling down the street—in as calm and leisurely fashion as if it were the middle of the day rather than midnight. She slowed her car, convinced her eyes were playing tricks on her. It had been a long time since Tyler O'Neill had been seen in this town.

As she pulled to a stop at the curb, he turned toward her, and her heart about stopped.

"What the hell are you doing here, Tyler?"

"Well, if it isn't Juliette Tremblant." He made his way over to her, then leaned down so he could look her in the eye. He was close enough to touch.

Juliette was not, repeat, *not* going to touch Tyler O'Neill. Not with her fingers. Not with a ten-foot pole. There would be no touching. Which was too bad, since it was the only way she was ever going to convince herself the man standing in front of her—as rumpled and heart-stoppingly handsome now as he'd been at sixteen—was real.

And not a figment of all her furious revenge dreams.

"What are you doing back in Bonne Terre?" she asked.

"The manor is sitting empty," Tyler said and shrugged, as though his arriving out of the blue after ten years was casual. "Seems like someone should be watching over the family home."

"You?" She laughed at the very notion of him being here for any unselfish reason. "Please."

He stared at her for a second, then smiled. Her heart fluttered against her chest—a small mechanical bird powered by that smile.

"You're right." But that cryptic comment was all he offered.

Juliette bit her lip against the other questions.

Why did you go?

Why didn't you write? Call?

What did I do?

But what would be the point? Ten years of silence were all the answer she really needed.

She had sworn off feeling anything for this man long ago. Yet one look at him and all the old hurt and rage resurfaced as though they'd been waiting for the chance. That made her mad.

She put the car in gear, determined not to waste another minute thinking about Tyler O'Neill. "Have a good night, Tyler," she said, liking all the cool "go screw yourself" she managed to fit into those words.

It seems Juliette has an old score to settle with Tyler.
Pick up TYLER O'NEILL'S REDEMPTION
to see how he makes it up to her.
Available September 2010,
only from Harlequin Superromance.

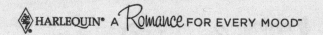

Watch out
for a whole new look for
Harlequin Superromance,
coming soon!

*The same great stories you love
with a brand-new look!*

Unexpected, exciting
and emotional stories
about life and falling in love.

Coming soon!